CHRISTMAS IN ASHES

CHRISTMAS IN ASHES

Written by

'The Oxenford Writers' Group'

Bren

Heather Mouy

Kathlyn Tedder

Luz Lleuful

Marge Norris

Nora Lleuful

Tedder Company PTY LTD
2015

First Printing: 2015

ISBN -10: 0994252609

ISBN-13:978-0-9942526-0-9

Tedder Company PTY LTD
37 Macquarie Ave, Queensland 4214, Australia

www.studiovillage.com.au

Dedication

This book is dedicated to the firefighters who work
courageously to extinguish the many bush fire outbreaks
experienced in Australia each year. Also to the many families
who've been affected by the nightmare of bushfire.

Contents

Acknowledgements

The Oxenford Writers' Group is a group of passionate writers who meet regularly to share and enrich their writing skills. I am grateful to each and every one of the members for their passion and dedication, which has been the driving force of this book.

We'd also like to acknowledge three home school students who participated in a few early discussion sessions.

Our thanks to the Studio Village Community Centre for its ongoing support as well the provision of a comfortable place to meet.

Kathlyn.

Preface

This book was inspired by the frequent summer bush fires that affect many Australian lives each year. The weather is usually unbearably hot and dry, the country often drought stricken. Rural Australians often enduring hardship as food and water for their animals becomes extremely scarce.

The residences' water tanks often run dry and many have to buy water to keep their own homes running. Water becomes a luxury.

In Victoria the drain on the electricity supply, as residents switch on their air conditioning is excessive resulting in frequent power cuts.

Bushfires are a natural occurrence in Australia however discarded cigarette butts, which had not fully extinguished, have started many of today's bushfires. Some have even been deliberately lit.

The fires often run out of control spreading rapidly across the tinder dry land burning at horrific temperatures. A subtle change in wind direction will change the course of the fire front and frequently takes people unaware. A raging fire can send burning embers up to 40 kilometres ahead of the fire front.

A member of our writing group had personal first hand experience with a fire travelling through her rural town. Her family was one of the fortunate ones to be missed but many homes in the district were destroyed. Her first hand recounts plus the media coverage on more resent bushfires gave us plenty   of   material   to   work   with.

CHAPTER 1   SMASHED

The heat of the last week had been unbearable. The local power cuts meant Jessica couldn't run her air conditioner. She opened the doors and was hit by a wall of heat driven by hot dry northerly winds. She closed them quickly. The temperature had been over 40 degrees for days now. Recently they had to buy water; the tanks had been completely dry. Today she could afford this one small luxury, a soak with her baby Benny, in a little kiddies' wading pool on their parched back lawn.

*****

He doubled over panting; the stomach cramps from running were intense. Harley was no athlete and running in leather boots was challenging in itself. In spite of the pain he started to run again, he could not afford to stop and recover. He glanced over his shoulder and scanned the horizon as he strode on, nothing… yet.

He'd travelled quite a distance already, initially on a stolen motorbike, before he heard sirens then tossed it in a creek. He'd hidden until the police car passed and had been running ever since.   All he'd seen for what seemed like forever was farmland.

He blinked twice, his luck was changing, three houses clustered together were just up ahead. Two were run down and old looking joints but the third… a palace. He headed straight for it.

The side door to the garage was open, he slid in unnoticed, no keys about but one very nice new car sat waiting.

He surveyed the area quickly and spotted the activity in the yard. '*Perfect timing*,' he smiled to himself as he stealthfully entered the open side window.

Harley frantically searched, all he wanted was the keys and he was out of here.

*****

Jessica and her baby had grown tired of the splash pool. Wrapped up in their towels, she carried her baby inside. To her astonishment Jessica glimpsed a seedy-looking stranger's reflection in the chrome toaster. She gasped and it was gone. She looked around apprehensively, nothing. She shook her head, the heat was getting to her, may be she'd just imagined it.

Her mobile phone burst into song, she answered it. "Hi Babe, I'm at Paul's. The goats travelled well. They're fine. They have plenty of feed here," came Matthew's loving voice.

"That is good news. When do you think you'll be home?"

Her attention was distracted there was a strange yet familiar noise, it took her a moment to realize it was the automatic garage door going up. Her mind was reeling. Matthew was speaking but she missed what he was saying.

He repeated, "I should be home in five hours. What time is the gourmet food for tomorrow's Christmas lunch being delivered?"

She thought she heard her Range Rover start up. Her heart skipped a beat, "How could that be?" she uttered. "Matthew there is something strange happening here. Can I ring you back?"

She disconnected the phone without waiting for an answer. She headed for the garage. Her body bristled. She suddenly inhaled. She was just in time to see her car heading backwards at speed down the driveway.

*****

His adrenalin was gushing to the max. Harley floored the accelerator. He was sixteen, unlicensed and had just stolen his fourth car.

"They're all going to burn in hell," he sniggered to himself, as he brutally shifted gears. "They all deserve to die."

"Got to get out of here real quick. Once that little fire I started kicks off the whole fuck'n place will be burnt to hell."

He gave a cruel laugh then turned to check the horizon for smoke.

As his eyes returned to the road there was a camper van coming towards him.

"Get out of the way asshole," he yelled and accelerated straight towards the on coming vehicle.

The campervan swerved but lost control. Before Harley could respond the vehicle swung madly around walloping straight into the driver's door sending Harley's car spinning airborne into the ditch. The campervan flipping and rolling several times before stopping wedged upside down against a gum tree.

*****

Raj opened his eyes. All he could see was blood. He wiped the back of his arm across his face. Shards of broken glass ripped across his skin. Painfully he made his way out of the smashed campervan.

He heard screams. His eyes searched for their source. He spotted a scrawny tattooed lad, on fire, crawling to the side of the road disheveled and disorientated. Raj leapt to his feet in spite of the pain in his ankle and rolled Harley on the ground extinguishing the flames. This boy needed medical help urgently.

The lad was barely conscious but Raj mustered up the stamina he required and over looking his own pain dragged him towards the nearby houses.

*****

Tom was in deep thought when he heard someone banging loudly on his front door. He had just finished a few of his chores and was totally surprised as he was a bit deaf and may not have heard the original knocking.

Thinking it was his wife Lilly, returning home after doing the Christmas shopping in town, he opened the door. He was shocked to see an Indian man covered in blood standing there.

There was a sudden rush of blood racing through Tom's veins and he blurted out, "What the hell is up with you?"

"Hold your horses. We were involved in an accident," the Indian said warily gesturing to his injured tattooed companion. "The lad's been burnt and hit on the head. I think he has concussion."

Tom looked over at the bloodied young lout and bristled.

"I don't want that low life here! Both of you get off my property at once, before I shoot you!"

*****

The young mother stared at her coffee cup. Her call to the police had been of little help, someone would be out later to take a statement. She didn't want to make a statement! She wanted her car back! She was stuck out here, without a car.

Knock, knock, knock.

'*Must be my young neighbor Vivian*,' she thought, smiled then opened the door.

Jessica stood mute as she struggled to comprehend the scene in front of her. The seedy face she'd seen in the reflection earlier was now standing on her doorstep, covered in blood. The blood ran from his head through his eyebrow and cheek piercings down his chest. His torn shirt revealed his multitudes of heavy black tattoos. The blood actually looked like it belonged over the exposed vial images. Amongst them the name 'Harley' was boldly written.

Pointing at the scrawl on his chest she snarled, "Is that in case you can't remember your own name, *Harley*? Or for the ambulance when they scrape you off the road?"

Harley rolled his eyes defiantly and shrunk away from her.

A movement behind him brought her attention to a second man, a middle aged Indian wearing blood covered executive attire with a tie.

"Lady, we need help," demanded the youth.

The look in his eyes struck her immediately, she could read pain, mistrust, arrogance and many other emotions she couldn't quite decipher.

"Which one of you stole my car?" she growled.

The Indian man shrugged and looked at the tattooed teen, "Miss, the boy and I are..." Jessica cut him off.

"How dare you! You have quite a hide! Breaking in here, stealing my car, smashing it by the looks of it then show up here asking for my help! I hope you rot in hell!" Jessica went to slam the door but Harley had put his foot in the way.

"Get out!" she screamed.

"Excuse me Miss," interrupted the Indian man politely, "My name is Raj. I am terribly sorry to intrude upon you in such a manner but as you can see this young man and myself have been involved in a car accident and we are both injured. We have no way of leaving without some help. I only ask that you call the ambulance and the police so that they may take care of this matter and we will happily leave you in peace."

The teen suddenly put both his hands to his head and leant forwards staggering slightly.

"Please Miss," Raj looked pleadingly to her.

Jessica exhaled loudly and relented, "Out on the lawn! Neither of you are to set foot in my house. Do I make myself clear?"

They both nodded and complied.

After a few minutes Jessica reappeared with a first aid kit and a phone. Harley was sprawled out on her front lawn groaning.

'Serves the bastard right,' she thought to herself.

She handed the phone to Raj and instructed him to call the ambulance and police as she began to administer first aid.

*****

Rebecca had heard a loud bang in the distance. Perhaps a car accident she wondered. Instantly she had a bad feeling in the pit of her stomach and looked for granddaughter, Vivian.

Vivian was only four years old and she was nowhere to be found. Rebecca felt anxious because she had the great responsibility of looking after her and couldn't do much from in her wheelchair. Rebecca had wanted to ask Jessica for help with her granddaughter while Vivian's parents were away but Jessica had always avoided talking to her. Tom Davis, her other neighbour didn't like her 'Chilean' family at all, just because of their nationality. Rebecca had tried her best to make friends with him and Lilly. It occurred to her the language barrier was a large problem it made Rebecca feel very isolated.

Now she had been left to care for her granddaughter on her own for two days. Vivian's parents were due back that evening as they wanted to be home for Christmas tomorrow.

Rebecca called out to Vivian again.

Vivian felt very frightened and confused when she heard the bang. She went to look for her mum; she couldn't find her. She felt very stressed.

She heard her granny calling and went to her. Her grandmother wanted her to stay with her for her own safety.

She didn't want to stay with her grandmother and had a tantrum. She ran out to see what was going on outside. The girl became worried when she saw the injured people on her neighbor's lawn. She approached cautiously curious to see what was going on but no one noticed her because they were too busy.

CHAPTER 2   TRIAGE

"Vivian," Jessica tried to smile as the terrified four year old approached her, "Sweet heart, I'm very busy making these men better right now. I need you to do a job for me, please," Jessica uttered anxiously.

"I can help you," Vivian replied.

"Thank you Sweetie. I need you take to a message to Mr. Davis across the road. Can you do that?"

"He scare me," Vivian muttered as she put her thumb in her mouth.

"Please, I'll share my jellybeans with you. Pretty please," Jessica beamed showing her the stash of jellybeans in her pocket.

Vivian took the note from Jessica and headed across to Tom's house. The old man was sitting on the front porch reading the newspaper. He looked up and saw the foreign child coming up his front steps.

"What is it ya little bugger?" Tom yelled.

Terrified the little girl dropped the note and ran straight back to Jessica crying.

Jessica hugged her. "Good girl," she said softly and offered her a handful of jellybeans.

Vivian stopped crying but she needed some water to drink.

"I can give you some water. I have got a bottle of water here," Jessica smiled at the little girl as she handed her another lolly from her pocket.

"Tank you," Vivian smiled as she chomped on a jellybean.

*****

Gradually recovering from the blow to his head Harley still felt very woozy and dizzy while lying still on the crisp lawn. His mind was racing his vanity got the better of him. He checked if his precious tattoos were damaged. Sighing with relief, his mind turned to his escape plan he had to get out of there it was only a matter of time before the fire he'd started would spread and he had no intention of being caught in it.

*****

"How dare that stuck up little nurse, demand I come and help her with that scum! Who does she think she is?"

Tom was a third generation farmer, it annoyed him enormously that yuppies like Jessica and her husband Matthew were building their super modern mansions and hobby farming on precious farming soil. Neither of them had any idea how to raise goats. He'd doubted they'd ever make any money out of it either. 'Glorified pets is all it is!' he'd often said to his wife Lilly. 'Wasting our valuable farmland on glorified pets.'

He looked across towards the chaos on Jessica's lawn.

"She wants me to help her with that rat pack! HUH! A no good, low life and another friggin' immigrant. It's bad enough having a migrant family next door. They're like a plague, spreading everywhere and you can't understand them. I wouldn't give either of them the time of day! I've got a good mind to go over there and tell her where she can stick this stupid note of hers."

The old farmer strode across waving the note in the air and opened his mouth to speak.

"Oh! Thank goodness you're here Tom," said Jessica looking up from the first aid kit she'd been rummaging through, "I desperately need a hand here."

"What!" the old man glared at the two injured men lying on her lawn, "Why would I bother waste my time on this pair. A ruddy foreigner and scum dragged out of a filthy sewer. This one'd steal your stuff the moment you turned your back on him!"

Jessica's face contoured in a way Tom didn't recognize and on cue her baby started crying from inside the house.

Before he could say another word Jessica had vanished

into the house.

"Yeah well I'm not about to leave the likes of you hanging around my place," The old farmer snarled at the injured teen, "The sooner we get you out of here the better." Picking up a bowl of disinfectant he began cleaning a wound on Harley's arm. He looked over at the Indian man, "Don't get me wrong, I don't like you either, what business have either you got out here anyway?"

*****

Rebecca felt panic she could hear the raised voices outside but she couldn't move because the child's Christmas craft was spread across the floor.

'She's spent hours making these decorations. I'd crush and destroy them rolling to the door with my wheelchair,' she thought to herself feeling defeated.

Rebecca looked at the shabby tree decorated by her young charge, so many angels and streams of tinsel over the lower limbs of the little old plastic tree. Overwhelmed by the frustration she yelled out for help but no one heard her. She made her way slowly to a nearby window and peered out. *'How peculiar, her neighbors and some injured strangers were in front of Jessica's house.'*

Rebecca felt alarmed. *'What about Vivian?'*

She started to pray because she believed that God would help protect her little one.

Will there be a miracle from God?

"Help her please," she prayed, banging her hands against the arms of her wheel chair. "I can't help much. If only I could get outside to look after my little angel."

*****

Raj clapped his hand to his chest. *Eeeer, eeeer* he wheezed.

Jessica looked up, and she stopped removing the glass shards from his arm, "You're asthmatic?"

Raj nodded as he wheezed.

"Where is your ventolin inhaler?"

"My campervan," he wheezed.

Jessica wasted no time; with her years of experience nursing in hospitals she knew the signs all too well.

"Tom I don't care what you think'" she argued emphatically, "It doesn't matter that he's Indian. He could be a purple alien for all I care but if he doesn't get his ventolin soon there's a good chance he'll die and I'm not going to allow this man to die at my beautiful home today. Now go!"

"Can't believe I'm helping that curry muncher," Tom muttered to himself as he drove his quad towards the overturned camper van. "What business does he have driving around here anyway? It's no tourist resort. Who ever heard of an Indian travelling in a campervan anyway? Blasted immigrants… taking over our country."

Tom pulled up next to the overturned camper van and studied the smashed wreck mangled into a gum tree. It was not going to be easy to get inside, the only two doors visible were severely buckled from the accident and facing upwards. Tom sniffed the air for any hint of a fuel leak. "Nothing," he sighed and approached cautiously through the shattered glass spread all around.

The only entrance left was through the shattered windscreen. Tom picked up a fallen branch and broke away as much of the remaining windscreen as he could. He climbed in cautiously trying to avoid the shards of shattered glass about him and squeezing himself between the steering wheel and the crumbled ceiling of the camper van. He made his way to the rear of the vehicle.

"Oh my god!" he uttered as the shock of the strewn camper hit him, "It's like looking for a needle in a hay stack."

He started digging in the rubble; broken plates, tins of food, an ornament of a boy with an elephant's head, clothing, a tie, toothbrush, business shoes and documents.

"Who goes on holiday with this sort of stuff anyway?" he muttered as he looked at the documents. "Tax department! What the heck!"

Tom quickly flicked through the documents. "I knew it! The curry muncher's a fucking tax auditor, sneaking around here on the sly."

Boom The whole vehicle rattled and shook from the impact as something struck it hard. Tom looked up; a massive gum tree limb now obstructed the smashed window he'd entered through.

He suddenly felt unsteady as pain struck him across the left side of his chest. He braced himself and searched his pockets for his angina tablets. Empty. He lowered himself into the rubble and waited for it to pass.

CHAPTER 3   HEATING UP

Tom shut his eyes and tried to distract himself from the pain. Lilly would be back soon with all the Christmas fare. She loved Christmas and would have the car loaded up with lots of wonderful presents for the grand kids. He warmed at the thought. She'd be up late tonight, wrapping presents and still get up early tomorrow to cook up a storm for Christmas. She always makes such a fuss when the family came together to enjoy a beautiful traditional Christmas lunch. To him Lilly was Christmas; she was his joy, his love, and his life. He smiled and felt the tension in his chest had eased.

Tom looked up at the rubble about him and immediately saw the inhaler he'd been searching for. He picked it up and made his way out of the vehicle. He bent awkwardly compensating for the collapsed ceiling. He pushed his way through the gum branches, which easily broke away, thanks to the stress of a long drought. He wasted no time returning with the inhaler.

Tom grunted at Raj, a prickly feeling washed over him as he glared at the tax auditor. The acknowledgement of the thanks Raj had tried to bestow on him was wasted.

Tom, still holding his chest had moved over to where Jessica had just wiped the blood off Harley's head.

She wanted to yell at

Harley still, '*What gave you the right to sneak into my house, take my car and destroy it*!' But she held her tongue.

Tom leaned down to whisper in her ear but the body language said there was tension between them.

Raj glanced across and wondered what they were discussing? He would have been surprised to know that Tom was warning Jessica that he had seen tax papers in the motor home and was questioning what is it this intruder wants up here.

*****

Rebecca's stomach had been tied in knots, she'd cried and cried and she thought to herself, '*What am I going to do? What will my daughter think when she gets back? I need to ring her but she is too busy with her business. And what about all the strange things going on in this place?*'

Rebecca was suffering with frustration and fear. She was feeling trapped in this little cottage with an enormous responsibility of being left with an active little girl in addition to the ongoing problem of barely understanding English. She felt helpless.

*****

Benny had become bored and finding himself alone set up a commotion, which made everyone swing their heads around toward the house.

"I've got to attend to my baby," said Jessica exhaustedly, as she turned towards the house.

"I'll give you a hand," said Tom, sounding awkward.

Jessica took his lead. "Thanks Tom," she replied, knowing full well he wanted to discuss the tax auditor in their midst rather than help her.

This gave the now trapped Harley his chance to escape. He had panicked when Raj had mentioned that he could smell smoke. He grabbed hold of Vivian's hand. He told the little girl they were going to play hide and seek. Momentarily she looked happy to play but then she looked closely at him and pulled her hand back.

Raj had been watching the sweet little girl. She didn't look like his little girl but her every movement made his heart ache with the longing for his own daughter.

The young lout grabbed her hand forcefully and started to pull her along with him. The little girl suddenly pulled to a halt.

Harley bent down closer to her ear and whispered, "What's the matter?" surveying the area for anyone noticing them.

"I don't like that grumpy old man. I don't want to go to his house," Vivian answered.

"Vivian," he tried to sound caring, "I'm here to protect you from the grumpy old man. Miss Jess told me to look after you. So lets go."

"Why are we going there?" Vivian enquired.

"To play hide and seek remember," Harley cunningly told his hostage as he continued towards the house.

She reluctantly followed.

Raj realized that Harley was up to something and followed them. He must get Vivian out of the clutches of that repulsive looking degenerate. He had to be stopped! The adrenalin was racing through his body now. The pain in his ankle hindered him.

Rebecca intuitively felt something was wrong. She frantically tried to wheel her chair through the maze of craft materials towards the unsteady make shift ramp, her son in law had made for her to get in and out of the house. Vivian was in trouble she could feel it in her bones, she just had to get to her. She had to look after her little angel no matter what.

The tattooed youth and Vivian made their way around the back of Tom's rugged, run down house. The back door was half open so, Harley pushed his way through with the curious little girl following behind. As they walked through the old place Vivian ran to the other end of the house.

"Come find me!" Vivian shouted from behind the fragrant pine Christmas tree.

"No, Vivian, I can't play that game yet," Harley, answered as he searched for Tom's gun.

Vivian stood staring at herself in a glass bauble on the tree. "Why can't we play?" she asked.

"We've got to do something very important right now," Harley, snapped at the disheartened four year old. "We need to find something."

Harley thought of a way to persuade his little detainee to help him, "It's a treasure hunt. If you find some bullets, I'll give you a treat."

Wide eyed she was staring at the pile of nicely wrapped Christmas presents placed under the tree, lifting her gaze she nodded then scampered about the house searching.

It didn't take Harley long to find the firearms cabinet. He'd broken into enough homes now to know where people hid them. The cabinet wasn't even locked. He picked up a gun and noticed the pile of ammunition sitting beside it. Delighted at his haul he called Vivian.

Stubbornly she refused to leave. She hadn't found her treasure yet and wasn't going without getting a treat.

Tension was intensifying in Harley rapidly, the cops were already chasing him and that do-gooder Indian had just let them know he was here. He had to leave, immediately! He grabbed the girl and forcibly hauled her out of the house.

Raj suddenly appeared.

Harley raised the gun to the child's head. Vivian started squirming and trying to pull away.

"I don't want any trouble here," he snarled, as he gripped Vivian firmly. "Do as you're told or I'll shoot."

Rebecca was making her way down the rickety ramp of her house to find Vivian. When she reached the road her heart nearly froze as she saw her granddaughter with a gun pointed to her head. Rebecca screamed.

"Shut the fuck up, old woman or I'll shut you up permanently!" he growled and he pointed the gun at Rebecca.

CHAPTER 4   RANSOM

"He wants money to give her back," wailed Rebecca, trying to speak enough English to be understood. "I look in my purse for money to get Vivian back." Rebecca began to frantically search through her purse.

"I don't want money you stupid woman. I want to get out of here. Get me a vehicle."

Rebecca cried desperately and pleaded with him in Spanish as English completely failed her now.

She had no vehicle.

She had little money.

She had nothing to offer him.

She just wanted her grand daughter back, alive.

Jessica heard the commotion and raced to the front verandah, holding her baby tightly. Tom followed close behind her. Fear struck her and she held her baby even tighter to her chest as she saw the tattooed scumbag, with a gun to little girl.

"What the!!??" gasped Tom as he appeared behind her.

Jessica tried to steady herself.

Benny felt the tension and squirmed in her arms. Jessica steadily rocked and calmed her son. All the while she was terrified. Harley beckoned them over. They walked towards the volatile scene.

The little girl focused on her grandmother intensely.

Rebecca tears streaming down her face, was speechless. Harley still had the gun pointed at her granddaughter.

Raj was not in sight. No one had seen him leave. No one seemed to notice.

Jessica felt torn between protecting her own baby and the safety of the sweet little girl whose life was now in peril. To add to the danger there was a faint smell of smoke coming from the valley below. She wished Matthew were there, he would know what to do next.

She thought she saw a movement from the side of Tom's house. *Was it possible Raj was hiding there?*

Harley obviously didn't know he was there.

What was he going to do?

How could he disarm Harley without putting Vivian's life at risk?

She turned to Tom. He was an off colour, his skin slightly greyed and his lips and under his eyes were bluer than they should be. Jessica knew the signs, he was putting on a brave face but his heart was distressed. He would need his angina spray. She suddenly remembered she had a bottle in her medicine cabinet. Lilly had brought it over a couple of days ago for her to take into the hospital. She wanted her to ask one of the doctors if he could take a stronger dose. She quickly told him where to find his medicine before they reached the scene.

Tom stepped in front of the young mother and baby in an effort to protect them.

The young villain shouted, "If you want this brat alive you'll have to give me some form of transport."

Tom said "Okay, Okay take it easy Harley just don't hurt the little girl, for god's sake! Wait a minute I'll get the quad."

He ran quickly to the shed rapidly trying to think of a way to foil him.

With trembling hands he emptied most of the petrol from the quad into a can, screwed the top on and wheeled the bike out to the front where Harley stood.

"Hurry up, Hurry up old man I haven't got all day."

"Okay here is the quad. I'll give you the keys in exchange I want you to let the girl go and throw the gun on the ground."

Grudgingly, Harley did so but first he removed the bullets with a smirk. He was a nasty piece of work but smart enough to know they wouldn't be able to shoot him without bullets, He tucked them safely in his pocket. Sniggered at them all and threw the gun to the ground.

"Throw the keys here Tom and I'll let her go."

The exchange was made and Vivian couldn't run fast enough to get away from the young villain and rushed into Tom's arms to his surprise.

Rebecca called out to her, Vivian ran to her granny, trembling and relieved.

Harley quickly started the quad and took off rapidly yelling foul abuse, as he did the finger at them all.

He tore off screeching around the corner of Tom's house. The group stood watching almost unable to move.

Wham! The sound of a massive impact from around the corner broke the stunned silence.

Tom told the others to wait while he checked to see what had happened.

The old farmer looked in disbelief, as there stood Raj rubbing his strained arm, a sledge hammer lying on the track behind the quad and Harley holding his shoulder driving the quad like a drunken maniac tearing up the path.

"Did you just hit that asshole with a sledge hammer?" Tom uttered shaking his head.

"Yip. Clipped him on the shoulder," smiled Raj, "That little creep deserved it."

Tom smiled at Raj, "Couldn't agree more. For a curry muncher you've got balls man," and slapped him on the back.

Raj smiled back. He had never expected this man to ever be friendly towards him. It was a nice feeling.

Tom's face suddenly returned to being stern as he remembered the tax documents he'd seen. He turned and watched as Harley continued riding off befuddledly into the distance.

CHAPTER 5   THAT MONGREL

Tom felt very pleased with himself. He boasted to Raj about emptying petrol from the quad, before giving it to Harley, trusting that he would get far enough away to cause him some irritancy when his journey suddenly stopped.

Raj took another deep puff on his inhaler. All this excitement had really stirred up his asthma but there was something else stirring up his asthma as well. Raj had pushed it to the back of his mind but it was becoming a niggling concern, the faint smell of smoke seemed to steadily be intensifying. He looked over to the crying little girl. Vivian had been through more than any little girl should. He would gladly give his life to protect his own daughter from such a horrific thing. He wished he could have done more to protect this little one. He fought back a tear. And stared at the little girl feeling intensely protective.

"Why is he looking at me?" Vivian whispered as she hugged her grandmother hiding her face from him.

Jessica looked at the exhausted group about her. A fragile old lady in a wheelchair holding a scared little girl, an old man looking a little pale and an injured middle aged Indian man puffing on an inhaler then felt her hungry baby wriggling in her arms. She'd never been all that neighbourly and certainly would never normally ask a stranger into her house but today was different. Jessica managed to let go of her desperate need to keep up appearances and invited the group into her home for coffee.

Raj took the initiative and pushed Rebecca's wheelchair up the driveway so he could use the little ramp from the garage onto the verandah, to get her inside.

Jessica turned to Raj as the shaken group were making their way into her kitchen and said pointing to her phone, "Would you ring 000 we need to let the police know where Harley is headed?"

She turned to Tom, "You need the ambulance to check you over as well."

Rebecca stared at the enormous and magnificent artificial Christmas tree displayed in front of her. Her mouth gapping as she cast her eyes across the elaborate decorations displayed throughout this immaculately furnished room. She could not believe that a family could live in such a grand place. She felt out of her depth, she had never been in Jessica's house although Vivian had visited often.

Raj returned quickly, he turned to Jessica, "The phone is dead!"

She looked at him startled. She felt alarmed at not being able to contact emergency services by phone.

Tom announced with a chuckle, "Don't worry about Harley he isn't going to get far I took most of the fuel out of the quad."

"Oh Tom! How could you! I don't want him back here! I was hoping I would never have to see his ugly face again!" She flung the words at Tom then stormed across the kitchen to make coffee and to calm down.

Rebecca asked Vivian what had happened in Tom's house. She shook her head and refused to tell. Rebecca feared it was too traumatic for a young child to explain.

The only consolation the old woman thought was that Raj had hit the despicable youth.

The old woman felt distressed because Vivian hadn't said anything she was only able to cry. She did not seem to understand what he'd wanted from her. The old woman cringed; she feared what may have happened to her little angel, alone with that vulgar degenerate.

"It is too much for her she can't handle it," she softly says as she cuddled her sobbing granddaughter.

Jessica asked Vivian gently, "What did you do with Harley?"

Vivian lowered her eyes and snuggled up onto her Grandmother's lap crying and said nothing.

"Vivian, she alive," she sighs holding her close and trying to focusing on the good outcome they had instead. She gives thanks to god.

"Darn, there is no electricity!" Jessica states as she looks at the clock, "Thank goodness my Christmas food hasn't arrived. It'd be spoilt without the fridge running… and its dinner time."

She turns to Tom feeling a little calmer now. "Tom do you think we have lost the electricity because of power cuts?"

Tom shrugs, "We'll just have to use your gas cooker." He says looking at the impressive sparkly new gas stove installed in Jessica's designer kitchen.

Jessica gets two saucepans from the cupboard and pours water from her bottled water dispenser.

"Benny's bottle is in the fridge but it won't last long without power," Jessica mutters as her thoughts return to looking after her baby.

Rebecca asks Vivian if she would give Benny his bottle. Her eyes brighten a little and she nods a reluctant yes.

"She would be able to look after the little baby and play with him," says the grandmother reassuringly as she reads the stress in Jessica's face.

Jessica looked at Raj limping over to assist her and let out a large sigh of relief as she realized she couldn't do everything and welcomed the help. Wasting no time Jessica directed Raj to make sandwiches for everyone with the odds and ends in her fridge and poured Vivian a glass of juice made the adults each a coffee then warmed Benny's bottle.

As Vivian and Rebecca gave baby Benny his bottle and the adults ate their sandwiches, Jessica tended to Raj's ankle adding a special bandage, which would allow him to walk on it with minimal pain.

She went into Benny's bedroom with the two children, who were soon both asleep.

"I'm glad all that's over," said Jessica as she flopped into a chair, sat down for the first time in hours, picking up her rapidly drying sandwich to take a bite.

CHAPTER 6   FUEL!

After the exchange Harley couldn't wait to get away. He'd straddled the bike and took off like a bat out of hell. His head was reeling. He couldn't believe his good luck. He felt like the king of the road, the early evening breeze on his face, an empty road and a bike under him.

"Wow, everything is going my way man. Easy peazy!"

The icing on the cake, his precious tattoos weren't even damaged. Being vain this was very important, part of his identity.

After about two kilometers the engine gave a coughing spluttering sound putt, putt, putt and came to a shuddering halt.

What the hell was going on?

What ever he tried didn't work and then the realization that he had been duped, and his rage was indescribable. He gave the useless vehicle a couple of vicious kicks and hurled it down an embankment scrapping his calf as he did.

He cursed as he walked away.

He was absolutely livid. His temple veins became prominent, his face turned a dangerous red and his eyes felt as though they were popping out of his head.

"How dare they! Those fucking, cheating bastards! I should have shot them when I had a chance. Screw them; they will regret this, big time! No one treats **Harley** like that!"

He stood there fuming if it were possible steam would be coming out of his ears. He had to sit down on the side of the road to think. Revenge was all he could dwell on. His heart was pounding with anger. At that moment he could have exploded with anger or had a heart attack. He sat with his head in his hands; he had often heard the word 'karma' mentioned. Was this 'karma'? His past was coming back to haunt him.

He had to rest from pure emotional exhaustion. He drank some water he'd found in an old discarded bottle tucked into the console with a pile of rubbish, then lay down for a while. His shoulder ached where it'd been hit, luckily it was only a little bump.

When he became more composed he realized he was quite far from town, his only option was to walk back. Traffic hardly ever passed on these country roads, ruling out a lift.

He started to walk; the road back was uphill making it even harder. Thank goodness his calf didn't pain too much. After walking about a kilometre he'd finally reached the edge of the plateau, he thought that he smelt smoke he looked behind him and saw the fire he'd started, coming up from the valley.

In no time the orange flames were spreading up the far away slopes like a hungry monster devouring anything in its path. It was mesmerizing to watch. Flames danced from one tree to the next, leaping across the distant road looking like delicate ballerinas. The most spectacular fire works by nature.

Harley stood there hypnotized. When suddenly he came to his senses, it was rapidly approaching the plateau, if he didn't run quickly; the flames'd soon surround him.

Panic overtook him. Could he out run this fire?

Instead of tranquility soon the trees would be like burning torches.

Little bits of tinder floated down. The smoke was taking the oxygen out of the air and making it difficult to breath.

He felt woozy and felt a large pang of regret as an ember bit his skin. The heat was unbearable.
"Oh! God what have I done?"

CHAPTER 7   SMOKE ON THE HORIZON

"I've noticed the smell of smoke is steadily worsening," stated Raj as he sipped his coffee, "Is that a problem?"

A frenzy of fears and panic leapt from one person to the next as the reality of being caught in a bush fire exploded in the room.

As Tom was a member of the local volunteer firefighters organization, he had the best knowledge of the local area. He made immediate suggestions on what they must do. The old farmer explained about a big old underground concrete water tank, which was built behind his house.

"No one knows what condition the tank is in, but it's our best chance of survival if the fire reaches us," stated Tom looking at the pale faces fixed on him.

"Tom did you say under ground water tank?" asked Raj, his face rapidly draining of what little colour it had left.

"Yeah mate. The underground water tank's the safest place we've got to survive a bush fire. Now you need to…"

Tom's words blurred out as Raj felt his world collapsing about him. Last time Raj was put in a confined space he became so panic stricken he nearly died of an asthma attack. The doctors' called it 'claustrophobia'. He wanted desperately to vomit.

Raj remembered the look on the little girl's face. Those big brown innocent eyes looked straight into his heart. She needed him to protect her. He was not going to let her down again. He steadied his trembling body as best he could and tried to refocus on Tom's instructions. He would do everything he could to keep her safe.

"…we would need to collect a few items for survival, emergency rations…" Tom looked intently at Raj. Raj understood the look; he was expected to be his right hand man, "… also we only have a small amount of time if the wind continues blowing this way, about an hour, is my best guess."

"Jessica can you get several large bottles of water for each person. A couple of blankets each, plenty of towels, food such as: canned tins, biscuits, bread, fruit, cordial or fruit juice, milk for the baby, torches, matches, some clothes, battery operated radio, any important personal papers you may want to save…" He barely drew breath and then continued, "Most important MEDICATION, band aids, antiseptic…"

*****

Jessica ran to Benny fighting the shivers of fear washing over her. Tears sprang to her eyes as she saw the two innocent children sleeping. She desperately wanted just to hold Benny tight, it may be the last time she'd be able to hold him, but there was no chance of either of them surviving if she wasted her precious little time that way. She felt as though her heart was being brutally ripped from her chest as she turned and raced to get the survival gear ready instead.

Jessica walked past the mirror in the hall catching a fleeting glimpse; she was shocked at the face that looked back. Tired, smudged with dirt, hair in a mess, make-up smeared. She went to brush away the grime and saw her nails broken, nail polish coming off. Somehow after the trauma with Harley it didn't seem important.

So much of her home ran on electricity and now it was useless. They had been using torches as well as a couple of battery-powered lamps Jessica had ready during the blackouts, since nightfall.

She was beginning to question how much of all the trimmings she'd been indulging herself in were really necessary. She didn't even have the most basic safety item a battery-operated radio.

Panic struck as she suddenly thought of the gas bottles outside. She wasn't sure but she thought Matthew had said she must turn off the gas bottles if ever there was a fire, but she didn't know how.

*****

Rebecca was suddenly feeling very sick.

"Could someone ring up to the ambulance for me," she asked. But no one was even listening.

Rebecca reflected for a moment; tears rolled down her lined face, as the sudden fear for Vivian's parents' safety hit her. They were driving home tonight and the smoke was coming from the direction they'd be travelling from.

"God if you are listening, please keep Vivian's parents safe, I can't do this alone. I'm too old and so useless now. Can you also help me keep little Vivian from harm, keep me well enough to care for her and please keep these new friends safe too."

CHAPTER 8   PUTRID

"Jessica, I haven't got time to waste explaining the situation," he directed a stare towards Rebecca, "can you explain to her what's going on and help her prepare?"

Somehow he felt responsible for their lives and started to take charge of the situation.

The young mother nodded and took a deep breath. Tom and Raj raced out the door, leaving her to deal with it.

*****

Tom and Raj headed straight to the entrance of the old tank, beside his backstairs. The concrete water tank had been built under the backyard many years ago, unfortunately movement in the earth had caused a few small cracks, which he'd repaired but didn't trust. So this tank would only be used when all his other tanks were filled, which hadn't been for quite some years now.

"Raj I haven't opened this tank in years. Well not since we put the big new plastic ones in."

Raj looked at the scuffed dusty plastic tanks nearby, they looked ancient to him.

"All the water off the roof goes to the new tanks not this old one. I'm pretty sure it'll be empty."

The two men appraised the entrance to the tank it was just a couple of metres from the back stairs of Tom's house.

Tom had collected a spade along the way and used it to clear the dirt from around the entrance lid. He tried to lift the lid by the handle but it didn't even budge.

 "Can you give me a hand lifting the cover off the water tank."

They both tried together and felt a slight shift but not enough. Tom used the spade and a rock from under the house and together they worked on levering it open. They struggled for a while and finally it came lose.

As the lid lifted the foul air that escaped overwhelmed Tom. It smelt like something died in there.

"Let's take a look then," said Tom as he gestured to Raj to climb in first.

"Tom I can't go down there," Raj swallowed hard trying to hold back the intense fear welling inside him.

"Come on Raj, I'll hold the ladder steady she'll be right. Here take the torch."

Raj took a deep breath, "Thanks Tom, you're very thoughtful, but it's not the dark…" he swallowed hard and looked Tom in the eyes, "…its just… I'm claustrophobic."

"Ah, is that all, plenty of room down there mate. She's a big tank. You'll be right."

"You don't understand, I'd rather die than be in a confined space," said Raj suddenly realizing the truth in his words.

Tom studied the frightened man before him. "Mate if it's that bad I'll just have to knock you out then."

Raj drew a sudden deep breath and smiled anxiously, "Thanks, Tom," and shook the old man's hand, "You really are a good man."

Tom looked away quickly. The pangs of guilt hit him. How could he have hated this man simply because he was Indian?

Tom slowly lowered himself into the tank and was aghast at what he saw. There were a
couple of dead rats floating in the water. His stomach heaved and he felt the sudden grip of despair at the sight that met his eyes. The water level was about hip height and it was extremely unpleasant standing in the rancid water.

"Oh God help us!" he said.

They didn't have much time to clean up. Raj lowered a bucket down and Tom filled it as they tried to get rid of the floating carcasses. They removed the vermin as much as they could. He felt helpless, but there was no time to dwell on his feelings, there was a fire they would have to deal with. There was the wheelchair to get through the opening and only a thin ladder leading down.

He suddenly felt light headed, reality hit.

"Okay we will need to get the provisions down here quickly," he yelled to Raj from the foul tank below. "We're going to need something to keep our supplies out of the water as well as to keep the little girl and old girl from drowning see if you can find something narrow enough to fit through the hatch."

"Raj can you also let everyone know
to wear comfortable clothes as it is going to be a bit wet for a while. Also let them know natural fibres like cotton and wool are best, they don't melt in a fire." His throat tightened on the words.

Raj looked from Tom's stern face to his filthy torn polyester shirt and then down to his lightweight polyester torn and bloodied business trousers. "This is all I have."

"Don't worry mate I'll get you some better gear. A pair of thick denim jeans and a heavy cotton work shirt with long sleeves will do you, perhaps an old jacket too to protect you from the fire. Might be a bit big, but it'll do you."

*****

Jessica was putting the emergency supplies out on her verandah when Rebecca joined her. As she checked through her supplies she explained to Rebecca that; she too needs to collect supplies for herself and Vivian. Rebecca didn't understand and argued they don't need anything else and it's still scorching hot. They don't need blankets in this hot summer.

Jessica soon lost her patience with her. She yelled at the crippled old woman, who was so upset that she wheeled herself back to her own house.

The young woman went and changed into Matthew's flannelette shirt and a pair of jeans. She was sorry she had yelled at Rebecca, but the circumstances were getting worse. She could see fire embers being blown around starting spot fires in the distance.

*****

Rebecca headed back to her house. It was hard to navigate the wheel chair around the unfamiliar terrain in the dark. She saw the glow of the fire on the horizon and felt a little panicked about the smoke intensifying.

"It's too far away to bother us here," she muttered to herself as she hastily turned the wheels of her chair, "These people are over reacting. They need their eyes checked. I'll be glad to be back home, away from them."

Her wheel chair hit a rock and started to wobble. Rebecca tried to steady the wheel chair but lost control. It ran off the path and into a garden bed. A dead branch jabbed her in the side.

Tears of frustration and exhaustion rolled down her face. She took out her handkerchief and wiped her face then recomposed herself before wheeling the rest of the way home carefully.

*****

Vivian smelt the smoke as she slept and dreamt of tasty marshmallows being roasted at a campfire.

CHAPTER 9   SPARKS

Rebecca raced her wheelchair about her home as she started to prepare for a possible fire but she couldn't lose the thought that these people were overreacting. First she closed all the windows after a few minutes she decided to ignore these crazy people and started wrapping a few Christmas gifts she'd hidden from her family.

She started thinking about Vivian and wished Jessica would just show compassion towards her too. She let Vivian stay at her place. Even after her encounter held at gunpoint by satin's tattooed son. She was still afraid for Vivian's safety, maybe she shouldn't have left her with that cold woman.

*****

"Jessica the tank's about waist deep in water. We are going to need to use your dining chairs to stop the little ones and Rebecca from drowning."

"What?" snapped Jessica feeling suddenly defensive, "They'll be ruined. Why don't you use Tom's chairs?"

"Tom's chairs are too big to fit down the tank entrance and I checked the old lady's house her chairs are metal. The metal will hold the heat," he looked up to see the tears of exhaustion and enormous anxiety suddenly rolling down Jessica's face.

Raj wrapped his grubby injured arms around her. "Jessica we're going to make it," he reassured her holding her a little tighter so she would not see the fear in his own face.

A sudden raspy noise escaped her as she drew breath. Raj knew he'd said the words she'd needed to hear.

She wiped the tears with her forearm and sighed, "Raj take them all. Take anything you need," and flew back into action with a new zeal.

Jessica pulled all her lovely new mink blankets, still packed in their storage bags, from her neat linen cupboard and headed for the front verandah with them.

Tom came bursting through her door, he was yelling, "Hurry we haven't got any time to spare. The fire will move rapidly across the dry grass once it reaches the plateau."

Jessica found it hard to accept that her beautiful house may burn. Nothing could prepare her for the possibility that they might lose their lives. Tom told her the blankets she had may be fancy but they were useless. He sent her off to his house for woolen blankets.

Tom stopped for a moment to grab a drink of water from the fridge. He gulped it down hurriedly. He could feel the adrenalin gushing. "What is it with these people?" he agonized, "Don't they understand the fire is a serious threat, we could all be burnt to death. Here's one fiddling about with stupid bags of useless blankets and who knows what the other is doing."

He looked about the room and suddenly realized none of these people had any idea of what is really going on. He slammed the glass down quickly, grabbed the medical supplies from the front verandah then headed for the water tank at a rapid pace.

*****

Vivian woke up and found Jessica rushing back through the door. She asked, "Did you make marshmallow?"

Jessica answered feeling bewildered, "I am sorry, no sweetie."

Vivian asked, "What is that smell? It is strong," wrinkling her little nose up.

Jessica answered the child trying to sound calm, "It is smoke from a fire."

Vivian started to cry. She was scared. Then asked, where is her granny, "I'm missing my Granny. Where is she?"

It was too hard for Jessica to explain to her about the smoke she was too young to understand what was actually going on. She didn't want to scare her either.

The little girl looked out the window and then asked, "Where did the pretty lights come from? Are they Christmas lights?"

Jessica was distractedly rummaging rapidly about her pantry.

Vivian was very curious and she said, "I want to see outside."

But Jessica is too busy and didn't hear her. Vivian headed outside by herself to look at the pretty lights.

CHAPTER 10   HOT SPOTS

Harley gasped for air. He'd been running as fast as he could for what seemed like an eternity. His throat was burning with dryness. He glimpsed behind him the flames were now licking the edge of the plateau. He'd been showered in smoldering tinder, most of which he'd managed to brush off before it'd burnt him but a few had managed to burn his bare skin.

There was no choice; the only chance to escape the fire had been to head back into the hostile community he'd just left.

'These people have water and would wet things down to stop the fire,' he'd thought to himself. *'All I have to do is find a hiding place and let them do all the work protecting the property.'* He laughed sadistically to himself, *'Serves them right, after treating me like shit.'*

He jumped the fence as he neared the properties carefully evaluating the layout for easy access to water and a safe place to hide. He darted about Tom's place remaining in the shadows. *'Too much activity there.'*

He headed towards the old woman's house.

'*That old bat is a walk over,*' he laughed as he stealthily moved about the outside of the property. '*Perfect a water tank behind the house and a shed butted right up against the house to hide in. They'll definitely be protecting this shed, if it was to catch alight the whole house'd go up.*'

Harley turned the water tank tap. The water gushed out. He gulped down plenty of water with great relief, and then quickly splashed some water on his burning arms and face, smudging the soot about his wounds.

'*My luck's changing,*' he grinned as he opened the shed door, '*...wasn't even locked.*'

Harley made his way inside the small shed moved a few tools about and made a space against the wall. There he could sit things out.

*****

Rebecca looked curiously out of her window. Something had caught her eye. She wheeled over to take a closer look. A wisp of smoke was rising from the leaf covered shed roof.

She wheeled quickly to the kitchen to get a jug of water. She opened the pantry and glanced about, the jugs were out of reach.

'*An ice cream container will do,*' her mind racing to stop the little hot spot before it became a fire.

She opened the cupboard and started frantically pulling all the appliances onto the floor trying to reach the containers behind, nearly toppling herself into the cupboard in her frantic search. Finally she grasped hold of a container then went to head for the sink but her wheel chair was trapped by the appliances, she shoved them out of her way and made her way to the sink. It was an awkward reach, the house had never been modified for a wheelchair and most times the family was there to help.

She turned on the tap and no water flowed out. *"Of course no electricity,"* she murmured as she frantically thought of another idea. *"The kettle will still have some water in it and there's cold water in the fridge."* She quickly drained the kettle and the near empty water jug into her ice-cream container.

Rebecca charged to the window with an ice-cream bucket of water sitting in her lap. She looked out the window to see a small flame had now appeared. She reached for the old casement window latch, which she'd closed a little earlier. In her haste it refused to open, she started to wiggle it. A sudden splash of water wet her legs.

The flames were rapidly spreading engulfing quarter of the shed roof. Rebecca felt her heart pound hard as she pulled at the latch, which finally surrendered. By the time she had the window open the furious flames leapt higher and now covered most of the shed roof. She flung her container of water at the fire, extinguishing a small patch momentarily.

She started screaming for help at the top of her lungs.

CHAPTER 11   COOPED UP!

Harley sat in the shed terrified as he could feel it was getting hotter and hotter. He had to get out unseen, but how?

The young fugitive heard the ongoing ear piercing screams coming from the Chileans' house. He decided it was now or never and bolted out of the burning shed, maybe he could redeem himself in some way.

Rebecca saw a blackened figure suddenly emerge from her shed coughing and gasping. She screamed even louder as fear gripped her. She couldn't identify him and thought it was the devil himself leaping from the flames. The petrified old woman continued screaming.

"Help me please, Lord. I don't know what to do!" she felt the enormous isolation enclosing. 'The neighbours' won't even hear my screams.' The devil ran away and nobody had even seen him.

The blackened youth dodged from sight quickly. He raced to the cottage door it would be a blaze soon too. Inside he saw Rebecca trapped by fear as he walked towards her. She escalated into a shrill scream of pure terror. He rushed over but couldn't stop her screaming, so he gagged her with a tea towel sitting nearby.

'That'll keep her quiet until she calms down a bit,' he

thought.

*****

Vivian had been outside enjoying the firelights in the distance. She decided to head home by herself in the dark and tell her granny about the pretty lights. As she approached her house she stopped stunned by spine chilling screams coming from inside, She saw the bad man who had wanted to shoot her creeping towards the front door of her house. She ran as fast as she could and hid in the chicken shed. She felt terrified and panicked. She saw the chickens in the shed, they were looking for some water to drink, they'd knocked over their water bucket. She didn't know what to do.

Vivian picked up her favorite hen, Sally and stroked her gently whispering words of reassurance as she nestled deep into the bedding of hay with the hen and tried to hide from the terror about her.

CHAPTER 12   FIRE STOPPERS

After changing into more fire retardant clothing Tom and Raj set to work and cleared as much rubbish away from the house as they could in the short time they had. Putting out the spot fires started by the falling embers as they went.

"Thank you sir, for all your help," the old man smiled to his assistant then shook hands with him. Tom's over sized jacket shaking on Raj's small frame as he did. "A noble gesture for a fair dinkum Aussie."

Raj saw the sincerity on Tom's face and felt a genuine connection to this man. He smiled at Tom in acknowledgement.

"Raj, we've got most of the rations ready to go down into the tank but we really need to stop the fires destroying our homes too. If we can't stop the fires we'll head down into the tank as a last resort."

The tank was the last place on earth Raj wanted to be, he was going to fight with every fibre of his being to save these homes just to avoid going into the water tank.

"I'm going to remove all the gas bottles and get any fuel drums I can find well away from our homes. If an intense fire engulfs them they'd probably go off like bombs.

I need you to keep putting out the spot fires and dampening down the area about our homes. As the fire gets closer more embers will fall, we need to keep on top of it."

Raj quickly followed Tom's lead and dampened his cotton shirt, splashed water from the tank on his face and grabbed the shovel. Little fires had started all about the place Raj frantically walloped them with the shovel, darting about like a man possessed; no fires were going to escape him.

Jessica glanced out the window; she could see the tax auditor across the road darting about putting out spot fires. She felt absolutely terrified about taking her son outside now that the sky had turned black with smoke and burning embers were falling from the sky. She picked him up and he must have sensed her fear, he began to cry.

She began to cry too she had always been such a composed confident person and now she felt like she was falling apart. She had put food and water in the stroller and Benny in the seat. She placed a couple of wet towels over her baby and a couple more over her own head. She opened the door, felt sick, took a deep breath and made a run for it. They had just reached Tom's place when there was a loud bang and there were flames emerging from the side of Rebecca's house.

*****

Raj stopped what he was doing. He hurried to investigate where the bang had come from. The now blazing shed had collapsed beside the house. Large flames were now racing up the outer walls of the Chileans' home.

He heard what sounded like a muffled scream and his stomach turned as he thought of that beautiful little girl being burnt. Adrenalin had his feet moving at lightening speed. He flung the door open to see a blackened Harley standing over the gagged old lady in her wheel chair. Before another thought could enter his head, Raj had leapt across the room and was pounding his fists with extreme hatred into Harley's already bruised and burnt torso.

Harley flung back with all his might; he'd been a street fighter for as long as he could remember. He pounded powerful blows into Raj's chest. Raj threw a punch fair into Harley's face, who yelped in surprise at the force of Raj's otherwise feeble punches. The two continued to fight, crashing into furniture and knocking over the little plastic Christmas tree.

Rebecca struggled to remove the gag. She finally loosened the cloth and screamed at the top of her lungs again.

All this commotion caused Tom to investigate. He marched in taking command, forcefully separating the two brawlers.

"We are in crisis and you two fools are fighting! We need every man's help this is an emergency!"

'I'll deal with this weedy little rotter later… if we are still alive,' he thought to himself as he stared at the sooty young brawler.

CHAPTER 13   STARVED OF OXYGEN

"I'm going to make this as clear as I can!" Tom roared, "There is a raging fire rapidly approaching, if we do not prepare ourselves RIGHT NOW, WE ARE ALL DEAD!" he paused and looked sternly into each terrified face. "DEAD! I hope I am making myself clear!"

The group silently nodded their heads. The scrawny Indian man brushed himself off and regained his normal composure. The rebellious teen glared at Raj then took a deep breath and looked towards Tom. " How can I help?"

"I want you working with me," he glared into Harley's defiant eyes, knowing full well the lad was only going to help to save his own butt. He would happily let everyone die for his own survival. "Raj I need you to bring Rebecca."

The old woman yelled "Yo mecesito urgente mi medicina por fabor,"she tried frantically to explain. She was so rattled she couldn't think of the words in English. She was resisting leaving, grabbing at furniture as Raj tried to move the wheel chair forwards. She totally refused to leave the house and clung on tight yelling.

The men exchange confused glances and then suddenly Harley blurted out "I understand her. What she wants is her drugs."

The old lady looked up and nodded. Tears rolled from her eyes, "Yes, drugs." She points to the upheaved cabinet that had her medicine stashed safely away.

"I'll get them," said Raj looking suspiciously at Harley then headed off.

Tom took over pushing the wheel chair and Rebecca tried to stop him again.

"That is quite enough! The building is on fire we cannot wait. Now behave yourself and lets get out of here."

They could hear Raj coughing as they headed through the front door and down the ramp.

*****

Benny was screaming in the stroller. She couldn't see him under the wet towels, but to stop could leave them unprotected. When she reached Tom's back verandah she threw back the towels. She lifted and hugged him to her. His screams became sobs, but when she had to put him down, to unload the water and food, he began to scream again.

Her body was running with sweat, the smoke was stinging her eyes. The smoky smell had gone down the back of her throat. She was exhausted and scared she just wanted to collapse on the ground. Jessica didn't know how she could continue. She felt so out of her depth then it hit her, she was reliant on her neighbours.

Clutching her precious baby tightly, she spun around and saw movement through the smoke haze near Rebecca's burning house. The group made their way to her refuge. She was suddenly surrounded by chaos. Rebecca was visibly upset, tears barely dry on her face. She was clutching a bag of medicine deifying anyone to take it from her. She was moving around in her chair trying to look beyond Jessica. Her stare made Jessica feel guilty about the way she had treated her earlier. But now she is looking at her in a strange way.

She was surprised when Rebecca screamed at her "Where is she? Where is my Vivian?"

She threw the words at her, "Did you leave her alone? How could you? She is just a little girl."

She was screaming with panic, "Where is she?"

No one knew were she was.

She cried out, "Vivian. Where is Vivian?"

Rebecca felt so responsible. She was supposed to look after her.

After taking her medicine she felt in control for a moment. She asked Jessica again, "Where is Vivian?"

Rebecca became furious with Jessica because she did not look after and care for Vivian, "What do you know about Vivian? Where is she now? She was in your house sleeping with your little baby. How could you lose a child?"

The old woman went silent. She glared intensely at the irresponsible young mother, "I will never trust you because you are not a good person and you didn't take care of Vivian. You are the worst neighbour I have ever met in my life."

She struggled in her chair as though she was willing her legs to work so she could search for her precious grandchild.

Jessica berated herself, *'How could she have forgotten Vivian? The last thing she remembered was something about cooking marshmallows.'*

Raj began to question Jessica and then before anyone could stop him he was off, searching for Vivian. Jessica turned to Tom for reassurance. He was deep in conversation with a sooty man who had his back to her.

Tom took a breath, coughed and continued talking to the stranger, "We are all going to have to work together, or some are going to die. I don't want to hear any more out of you. Take these wet bags and put that fire out, before it spreads," instructed Tom. "It doesn't matter what has happened before. The fire front will reach us soon, if we don't stop it our homes we will be burnt down and maybe us as well. I need you to be a man, examine your conscience. Try to put others before your self. Man up."

The stranger shook hands with Tom and without turning, headed towards Rebecca's house to do what he was told.

Suddenly a small blessing, the wind turned and the flames over the house began to shrivel burning back on itself.

Before Jessica had a chance to ask 'who the man was', Tom threw instructions at her. "We will put the water in beside Rebecca. She can hold your baby on her knee and you will have to push her across to the tank entrance."

With that Tom began to load the water containers he'd filled earlier, placing them around Rebecca.

Jessica could feel the animosity rolling off Rebecca in waves. Rebecca put out her arms to take her baby. Jessica was horrified. What if she dropped him or the chair tips over? Benny would be trapped under Rebecca's body.

Tom yelled, breaking into her thoughts "Hand the baby over; or risk him dying!"

She did what she was told and just as she put her hands out to push the chair the blackened man turned to face her.

Jessica screamed at the top of her lungs, "YOU, what are YOU doing back here? This is all your fault! If you hadn't wrecked the cars we could have been out of here. You bastard! How dare you come back here haven't you done enough damage already?"

CHAPTER 14   BIGGER ISSUES

Harley, escaping Jessica's fury, had offered to help Tom to put out spot fires and had quickly leapt into action. They had no power to run the pumps so their feeble efforts were limited to using wet sacks and shovels.

Tom wiped his brow and saw that Harley was tired, and wet with sweat but was relentless in fire fighting. Tom gained a little respect for Harley and felt there was a glimmer of hope for this lad yet. He went over to him and shook his hand.

"Thanks for your help. I couldn't have done it without you. You are not so bad after all." Then gave him a manly hug.

Harley felt a warm feeling inside. Something he had never felt before, he could grow to like this man. No one had ever had ever bothered to say thank you to him, let alone give him the time of day.

This other feeling that he experienced he wasn't so happy about now. Perhaps it was guilt. Something he'd never given a thought to. What had he done to these people's lives?

"We'd better help everyone get into the tank soon; the fire front has turned and is approaching again. There's so much to do and so little time."

They ran back to Tom's backyard the two women and a baby were standing around and not quite sure how to proceed. Tom took the lead and started to organize them.

*****

Raj flung open every door, every cupboard upheaved furniture he was absolutely frantically ransacking Jessica's home trying to find the precious little girl who'd gone missing. His throat was sore from yelling and inhaling the dry air. He took another puff on his ventolin inhaler. He felt an unsettling fear for the child's wellbeing.

"That sleazy scumbag has taken her as revenge!" he yelled out, to the empty house. "He's hidden her somewhere. I'm going to beat him senseless this time until he tells me where she is!

*****

The wind was steadily bringing the fire closer.

Vivian was reassuring the chooks quietly when suddenly a snake came out from its hiding place.

She quickly swung open the chicken coop door and ran off still holding her favourite chicken. Running away from the fire and snake as fast as she could and yelling for help as she ran.

Her thongs tangled in the grass and she fell. Sally flew away. She couldn't see well in the dark. She didn't know where she was. Wild kangaroos, wallabies and other animals were running past her, away from the fire.

Vivian lay on the ground sobbing.

CHAPTER 15   TUG-A-WAR

"I have turned all the house upside down searching for little Vivian," Raj locked eyes with Harley, "she is not here."

Either Harley's eyes could lie as well as his tongue or he genuinely did not know she was missing. Raj held back the raging anger that wanted to destroy this vile young man. He had to be sure before he lashed out.

"Do you know where she is?" he said holding his gaze on Harley's eyes.

Harley genuinely looked confused at this question and answered a hollow sounding, "No."

Raj had spent many years working with people's accounts and their many financial secrets. This boy was either the best liar on the planet or genuinely had no idea where the little girl was.

He turned to Rebecca, tears streaming down her face. "Where does she like to play? Does she have any special hiding places?"

Rebecca could hardly form a word, " animals, she like animals…" her words broke into a flood of tears.

Raj raced off hurriedly for the animal enclosures he'd seen earlier at the back of their home.

Benny started crying too, his chubby arms outstretched towards Jessica. He looked at her with such a look of need on his tiny face. Jessica put out her arms to take her son from Rebecca's lap, but the old woman tucked her arms firmly around the little boy glaring spitefully at his mother.

"You cannot have your son, why should you have your baby safe while my little granddaughter is missing?" Rebecca clutched fast to baby Benny stubbornly refusing to return him.

Jessica felt sick as she could tell from the look on Rebecca's face she meant everything she'd said.

Rebecca reverted to speaking Spanish and Jessica no longer knew what she was saying to her, but by the fierce look in her eyes and the way she spat the words aggressively towards her, she would bet she was being sworn at. Rebecca was getting herself so worked up she was becoming hysterical.

Jessica just needed to get her baby back. She slapped Rebecca across the face making her release her hold on Benny. The young mother hastily swiped Benny from the old woman's arms. A wave of relief washed over her as she looked into her little boy's blue eyes.

Harley and Tom had started lowering the supplies into the tank. Harley being younger offered to help lower all the provisions. Once the young man was inside Tom attached a long rope to the chairs one at a time and gradually they lowered the necessities down. The chairs had to be roped together as they were not stable enough in the water individually.

There was a lot of squawking going on above ground. The sooty refugee imagined what they were saying.

"Stop acting like a bunch of kids," he'd heard the old farmer yell. "We can't let him burn to death. We're not murderers."

Once down there Harley was splashing around in the water, things kept floating away and had to be secured. It was a real challenge.

"Come on we can't take too much longer. Hurry!" Tom shouted as he went down to check on the progress below. He saw Harley bending down and coming up with something in his hand. A knife in Harley's hand!

The old farmer made his way down the ladder into the tank then yelled, "What the hell do you think you are doing?"

The lad was startled as he wrenched the knife away from him.

He was furious, "So this is it, back to your old ways. I thought we had sorted things out. I thought I could trust you."

Harley was taken aback. *'What was wrong with the old man? Why was he so angry?'* He smoldered inside he was beginning to trust this man and had started to open up to him. *'Now he is turning on me. I was a fool to let my guard down.*

Huh!' Harley tried to get a word in edge ways but Tom was too riled up.

"We told you that he couldn't be trusted Tom!" Jessica chipped in her grievances through the opening above.

Finally Harley screamed above everyone, the sound echoing furiously through the tank, "Let me explain! You have got it all wrong! I'd noticed that one of the chairs wasn't secure and was about to cut a piece of rope to fix the problem." He pointed to the issue.

Tom drew a deep breath, "Sorry, I was too quick to judge you. Thank you for taking action. Someone could have drowned if you hadn't"

The lad suddenly felt awkward. No one had apologized to him before. Maybe this old man was different to all those he'd known before. He shrugged it off quickly and resumed the task at hand with an unfamiliar sense of being valued.

*****

Rebecca's hysteria and Spanish curses were still raging she was very angry with Jessica.

"If you don't stop your hysteria I'm going to slap you again."

The crippled woman went silent and turned the back of her chair on Jessica. An eerie silence settled between them.

CHAPTER 16   BUMPY PATH

Finally the people and fresh water bottles had to be lowered. Tom thought he'd leave Rebecca for last, as she had the most difficult personality. Exhausted as she was, she was still screaming for Vivian who had not been found.

Rebecca demanded Tom unload her wheelchair. She spoke Spanish and English entwined. She was determined she should find Vivian. Tom tried to convince her to head to the tank entrance.

Rebecca pleaded, "Tom you have to search for Vivian! What if she went back in our house looking for me? It's on fire, she could be dead!"

Tom tried to ignore her then replied softly, "Raj would have searched through your house before it became fully ablaze. I know he will keep searching until he finds her. When Raj finds Vivian we need to know where you are because the little girl will be scared and she will need you."

He was hoping that she would move to the opening of the tank at least closer to getting in in a hurry.

"I should be searching for her too," Rebecca responded.

"I cannot allow you to head off in a wheelchair in the dark amongst smoke and falling embers!" Tom yelled in frustration. "You will just have to do what you are told. And that means all of you." He said looking across at the young mother. "Now head to the tank opening, Harley is already over there he will help you unload the water bottles into the tank and believe me we have to act soon."

Tom picked up a couple of water bottles and headed down into the water tank to do a final check everything was ready for the group to settle in.

Jessica took Benny and made a dash towards the opening.

She was about to get into the tank first but she would have to change him, there was not going to be anywhere to change him in the tank. She looked toward her house trying to gauge how much time she had before it would be too late and they would be caught in the fire. What she saw froze her to the spot, the fire had come around behind her house and the sky was now glowing.

Frantically she lay Benny down and whipped the sopping wet nappy off him replacing it quickly with a fresh nappy from her nappy bag and headed for the tank.

Raj and Vivian were not back yet.

The wheelchair bound woman gave a sudden scream of frustration, "I'll find her myself," She dropped all the water she'd been carrying and wheeled off to go and look for Vivian.

"Raj is still looking for her, but he hasn't returned yet," she babbled as she rolled off, wheeling over rocks along a bumpy path almost falling from her chair. She didn't even know where she was going but she could not sit back and do nothing any longer. Her beloved Vivian was lost and the fire was closing in.

Tom peered out of the tank opening to see what all the commotion was about just in time to hear Rebecca's wheelchair overturn.

As she lay on the path with her wheel chair twisted about her legs Rebecca looked up and noticed Jessica's house was on fire too, she needed to tell the others. She panicked and yelled, "The house is on fire."

*****

Vivian was running to the creek chasing her pet chook. She'd finally seen her through the smoke and chased after her.

"Sally's thirsty."

Vivian started to climb down the steep creek bank to get her some water when she slipped and fell down the embankment. The stressed chook flapped away. The little girl felt frightened. She tried to climb out. The banks of the creek were very slippery. She couldn't get a good footing on the creek bank, her thongs didn't help and she kept slipping back down. She wiped her face and got mud in her eyes. She tried to clean the mud out of her eyes. She couldn't see where she was. She was trapped. She yelled for help, but nobody heard her.

The little girl was exhausted and had no idea how to escape she curled into a little ball and sobbed.

CHAPTER 17   A DARK HOLE

Tom was desperately trying to keep everyone safe, he was sweaty and apprehensive but he had to stay strong and in control of his feelings, the fire was coming closer and closer. Little embers were landing all about them now some bursting into small flames. He looked around for someone to help him rescuing the old woman, Harley was still in the tank below, Jessica and Benny were huddled under the stairs nearby avoiding the falling embers and Raj was still out searching for the four year old girl; the poor old lady was still upheaved in her overturned wheelchair and unusually silent. A shiver pricked his spine.

Jessica just clung tightly to Benny and watched as the rest of her house exploded into flames. *'How could possessions have taken over my life?'* she wondered silently.

She would've given everything she had left to know Matthew was safe.

Harley was feeling pretty proud of himself.   He'd organized a safe spot, a haven for little Benny where he couldn't fall in the water and drown. He'd even thought of Rebecca, he was sure they wouldn't be able to get her wheelchair in, so he'd rigged up a spot for her as well.

He couldn't believe what he just did, thinking of others instead of just looking out for number one. He had to admit it felt good.

Tom was yelling directions down through the hole. It wasn't easy to hear, his voice was echoing off the walls. Something about sending Jessica and Benny down first. Harley could hear Tom yelling to Jessica. He popped his head up to see what the commotion was about.

"Harley I need your help we're going to have to get Rebecca back in her wheel chair quickly and ready to go into the tank, before she catches alight."

He scrambled out of the tank and made his way towards the upheaved old woman.

Tom and Harley felt deep compassion for poor Rebecca. As they approached they heard her crying softly. The old woman was very frightened by the predicament she was in. She was very distressed; as she'd seen everything she held dear being destroyed before her own eyes. She felt incredibly frustrated at her inability to communicate the most basic of things to those around her.

Dodging the falling embers the men hastily returned Rebecca into her wheel chair, Harley barely righting the chair, as Tom placed Rebecca in its seat.

"You are so strong, lifting me back in the wheelchair," she said softly as she placed her hand on Tom's, "I thought I'd die there. Thank you, Tom."

Harley pushed the chair as fast as he could back across

the rugged terrain dodging the embers and small fires. Tom followed close behind. Rebecca never realized it was Harley who'd pushed her because she couldn't see behind her.

"How am I going get down the tank?" she mumbled frowning at the small opening.

"We'll send you down once Jessica is down there to assist you."

The old woman cast her eyes towards the young mother she now hated. She doubted she could trust her to help her down into that great hole. She was certain she'd be drowned and that heartless young woman wouldn't care.

Tom turned to Harley and said, "I really need you young man. We'll both have to work together to get everyone down."

Then turned to Jessica, "You will have to come out from under the stairs we have to get you and the baby into the tank."

She was frozen with fear, how could she take her baby into that filthy place.

"Hurry up, we don't have all day!" Tom yelled

It got her moving.

He sent Harley down into the tank first then yelled down to Harley, "Jessica is on her way, I will hold on to the baby till she's half way down. You reach up from the bottom, then she can pass the baby over to you to hold while she climbs the rest of the way down."

"NO, NO!" Jessica screamed uncontrollably, "I will take my own baby down!"

Tom simply glared at her intensely then demanded she hand over the baby.

'I'll let him help me,' she thought to herself, *'but if Tom thinks I'm going to give my baby to that tattooed freak he's got another thing coming.'*

She acted calmly and reluctantly handed the baby over to Tom and began her decent into the tank. She paused after a couple of rungs to tell Tom there was a large piece of canvas under the stairs that he might need later, then continued down. When she was chest height with the opening, she reached for her son. Tom handed him over.

Harley was behind her ready to take the baby. She wouldn't hand him over. She tried to come down the next rung but the baby sensed he had lost his security and threw himself backward. Try as she may she couldn't hold him. She screamed as the baby fell toward the murky water at the bottom of the tank.

Harley quick as a flash moved under the baby to catch him.

Amazingly Benny thought the whole thing was very funny and his laughter vibrantly rang around the tank. As the tattooed teen hugged the giggling baby a tear rolled down his face. Jessica was so relieved before she knew it she was hugging the rebellious youth with gratitude. She amazed herself after the ill feeling that had existed between them.

He sniffed up any remaining tears then proudly showed Jessica the safe haven he had made for the little boy. It was then Jessica noticed the huge blisters forming on Harley arms he was going to need treatment.

Tom yelled from the top, "Harley get your ass up here now there is no more time!"

The lad's feet hardly touched the ladder and he was out.

"Harley you will have to help me get Rebecca down the hole. I can't do it alone."

"Okay Tom. How are we going to do this?" he asked.

The old farmer pointed under the stairs, "Maybe we can use the canvas that Jessica mentioned was under there."

Rebecca was taking no notice of what anyone else was doing her eyes were fixed on the horizon searching for the missing child.

Tom yelled down to Jessica "We are going to lower Rebecca down in that canvas you saw. We will lower her all the way into the water. You will have to get her out, okay?"

" Yes, Tom what ever is necessary."

The old woman was so upset and emotional about her missing child. Rebecca was terrified, she'd never trusted being out of her wheelchair, let alone going down a water tank, especially with that unfeeling over indulged young mother. She felt helpless.

When she heard Harley was involved in her descent she lost it, crying hysterically, she was petrified of him. She definitely didn't trust him to lower her safely. She'd probably be dropped into the foul water and drown. Her vulnerability engulfed her and she became unable to speak. She was still trembling from the many earlier incidents.

"She didn't look after her; I can hardly expect her to look after me now! At least she has her baby. I don't know where my Vivian is, if she is safe or even alive," she blamed Jessica and then surrendered to her helplessness.

Tom said, "We need to get you down the tank now or we won't have any time left to find Vivian."

They wrapped the canvas around her and tied the ropes at each end. Harley helped ease her legs through the hole and then Tom let his end down and slowly they lowered her down carefully into the water. Jessica was there to release her out of her cocoon. She used the water to keep her buoyant.

As she unwrapped the canvas she was shocked to see the state of Rebecca's legs, she had been badly burnt. Her nursing instincts suddenly kicked in.

She was impressed how Harley had set up a rope to help

her get Rebecca into the place he had arranged especially for her. She quickly secured the old woman to the special chair and returned to little Benny.

Rebecca sat, almost detached to her surrounds, whispering desperate prayers, "God save us all."

CHAPTER 18   HIDE AND SEEK

"Vivian!"

Raj was in agony he'd screamed out for Vivian for so long his vocal cords strained as he yelled her name yet again.

"Vivian!"

His lungs burned with the dryness and he'd over used his inhaler trying to keep his asthma at bay.

"Where could she be?" he muttered to himself trying to peer through the dark smoky air about him. A few small fires lit the ground for him but Vivian was nowhere to be seen.

He'd looked through all the animal enclosures behind her home. He'd released the dogs and horse from their enclosures but the chicken coop was already empty and the door left open. *'Vivian must've let the chickens out but where would she have gone after that?'*

He'd returned to her blazing home and ran through the fire inside checking she hadn't gone back to her home. He felt his ankle pain and the singed skin on his face as he recalled the horrific scene and was glad she wasn't there. A wave of exhaustion washed over him but he could not surrender to it, she had to be found.

"Vivian!" he yelled into the smoky night sky. Feeling incredibly disappointed and frustrated.

Raj was now wandering aimlessly about, dodging the embers as they showered down and the many small fires that had sprung up about him. It was too late to bother putting them out. The only thing he could do now was find the little girl and keep her safe.

"Vivian!"

*****

Vivian had spent some time curled up and sucking her thumb feeling lost and frightened as she'd huddled in against the cool mud of the creek bed. She'd seen wallabies hop through the creek bed leaping quickly up the creek walls. She wished she could jump like a wallaby and leap right out too, but she was stuck.

Many birds had flown past squawking and flapping in fear. Vivian sensed the fear too. She wondered where her chickens had gone. Were they scared too?

She looked about for a tree to climb so she could get a better vantage point to see her chickens. She could see an old tree limb hanging down a little further up the creek bed. She made her way towards it, carefully stepping through the mud and rocks about her. The limb was nice and thick with a few branches to grab hold of. Vivian took a hold and pulled with all her might and lifted herself up onto the limb. She started climbing up higher calling for her chooks as she looked about for them.

"Here chicky, chicky, chicky, where are you?"

She heard nothing. Vivian started screaming and crying out because she was at the top of the tree now and was scared she was going to fall. The smoke was so strong it made Vivian feel disorientated. She started coughing.

*****

"BANG! CRASH!" an all mighty explosion broke the roar of the approaching fire.

Raj's felt ill as he realized it had come from the direction of his camper van wreckage. His petrol tank must've exploded. He gulped feeling the inevitability and sickened at the thought of the little girl alone in this living terror.

"Shiva, god of destruction, it is me you want, please let the little girl live!"

As the despair washed over him he thought he heard a sound, perhaps a distant scream.

Raj ran as quickly as he could ignoring the pain in his injured ankle and the many burns, bruises and abrasions he now had.

"VIVIAN!"

"Help," came a little voice nearby.

Raj ran past the tree Vivian was perched in, looking for her. He searched about calling her name but couldn't see her.

'Am I hallucinating?' he wondered.

Vivian screamed from above, "Help me please, I want to get out of the tree!"

Raj climbed the tree awkwardly. He was never good at climbing and it was even more challenging with the injuries but he was not going to let this little girl perish.

Vivian asked him, "Where is my Granny?"

"I'll take you to her now," he smiled.

He saw she was covered in mud and had a few minor burns but she didn't even complain. He took off his thick coat and wrapped her in it to protect her. They started walking back towards the houses. Vivian was tripping over trying to avoid the little fires all about them. Raj suddenly noticed she'd been wearing thongs and her feet would be easily scolded if she didn't step carefully.

He picked her up and made his way rapidly over the hostile grounds back towards the others.

*****

Harley looked at Tom squinting his eyes with a curious look.

"Tom you look like you're O.D.ing. What's wrong?"

"Oh, I wasn't going to alarm you but it's all getting a bit much for me, Harley," said the old man as he clutched his chest, "We had to get everyone into the tank before I could rest." He looked about him, "I only hope we survive this. We've really only got Buckley's now lad."

"What do you mean Buckley's?" asked Harley looking puzzled.

"Well, Lad," said Tom as he smiled at Harley, through his pain, "Buckley's hope means there is almost no hope at all, a miracle is our only hope."

Tom looked into Harley's eyes seeing the boy understood his meaning.

"I only wish, I had more time to teach you. I think you're a fast learner and you'd do well to have an old man like me, teach you some of his old tricks."

Harley smiled at Tom and felt an involuntary tear well in his eyes. "I'd like that too."

Then the massive pang of guilt gripped him so tight it burned through to his soul. His stupidity and selfishness was likely to cost him this friendship and his life.

Harley looked away.

He looked up again; he thought he saw a figure through

the smoke, lit by the glow of the little fires.

"Is that Raj?"

"Well I'll be, it looks like Raj and the little one," said Tom clapping Harley on the back.

CRACK BOOOOOM!!

A burning limb dropped off a tree and Raj and his bundle were gone.

CHAPTER 19   TRAPPED

Harley was running like the wind before he could think. He'd never done a good deed in his life. Here he was running to save a man who'd happily have killed him earlier that same day.

"Buckley's," he whispered to himself, "Go'na die anyway."

He reached the fallen limb to find them trapped and alive. The burning limb had landed on Raj's back and Raj had landed on top of Vivian. She was trapped by the weight above her. As fire danced across the Raj's back he tried to free himself using his arms but to no avail.

The young man grabbed the flaming limb and lifted it. Vivian wriggled free. Harley rapidly patted down the flames that now danced across the coat Vivian was wrapped in. He reached out to Raj.

"Take my hand buddy, I'll pull you out."

Raj looked up at Harley with a look that sent shivers down his spine. He knew the words he was about to hear. He desperately wanted never to hear them.

"It's too late. Take the girl and leave me."

"It's not too late!" he yelled and leapt into the flames and pulled wildly at the limb again. Then stepped back crushing the new flames off his clothing.

"You must save H E R!" Raj's words betrayed his pain.

Harley looked into his eyes, his face askew, asking Raj his forgiveness, but no words seemed to reach his lips.

"I believe in you. It's too late for me. Save the little girl."

The young man swallowed hard, turned grabbed the little girl and ran as though he was running from hell itself.

Vivian fought and kicked him, "No you're not taking me. Leave me alone. You're a bad man! Put me down!"

He barely noticed the little girl's assault he felt so much pain as the image of Raj's dying face was burnt into his mind.

The four year old started crying, "My chicken is gone and I want my granny. Where is my granny?"

The youth tried to calm her down and said with a giant lump in his throat, "We are going to see your Grandma now, don't cry everything will be fine."

As he ran he thought he heard a final deathly scream, which was almost engulfed by the roar of the fire. A cold shiver ran down his spine. He felt a pain deep in his heart like a shard of glass had just speared him.

The youth happily handed the little girl to Tom. He gasped for air after his sprint through the fires. She was covered in dirt and mud, had a few minor burns and bruises, but she was alive.

Vivian saw her grandmother's empty wheelchair and screamed in horror. "Where's my grandma?" She started kicking and punching Tom with all her might. "What've you done to my grandma?"

Tom struggled to point to her grandmother, through the tank's opening.

Vivian rushed down the ladder and leapt into her grandmother's lap snuggling in so tight the old lady could barely breathe.

She was so excited that her charge had returned safe and well, "Alleluia, she is alive!"

While the rejoicing was going on Harley explained to Tom what had happened.

Tom embraced him and said, "You did well, lad."

The pain of guilt intensified to an unbearable magnitude through Harley. Tears he'd never shed before in his life bubbled to the surface. There was no holding them back.

Tom spoke soft and reassuringly, "Raj died a hero and will be missed by his friends. He got his wish. He'd rather die than face his claustrophobia."

Very unlike Harley he said a little prayer, then followed Tom into the water tank. It was almost too late but they made it. The intense heat outside was becoming overwhelming.

CHAPTER 20   DEEP WOUNDS

They had been plunged into total darkness, except a small hole, which had once been where the water pipe fed into the water tank and was now a small window to the approaching wall of flames.

The unpleasant smell of the stagnant water they stood in was foul. Jessica stifled an urge to vomit. The slightest sound seemed to resound forever as it echoed off the walls around them. Rebecca's joy at the return of her grand daughter seemed to fill the void.

Several minutes flew past, they seemed like hours.

Harley suddenly sparked a lighter, which gave them some light. Jessica fumbled through the stash in front of her, pulling out a candle, which he lit and returned to her.

As her eyes adjusted to the dim light, Jessica saw the six glasses of water she'd poured earlier in anticipation of them all being in the tank. She knew they would all be suffering from dehydration.

Harley had craftily tied the chairs together creating a dry place for their belongings to be stowed and Jessica had made use of a small plank he'd secured above water.

Vivian didn't seem to notice her surroundings she was so

over joyed at her return, she continued, "I was on top of a tree and screaming '**help**'. It was God's miracle and I saw the nice man go past, where I am, in the tree and he help me get down."

Her Grandmother was listening intently to her, cuddling her tightly as the little girl told her story. Rebecca was so happy to be reunited with her and they both said a prayer together.

Jessica began to hand out the glasses of water she had one left over. She looked at Tom, "Where is Raj?"

He shook his head, "He was very brave but he is gone."

He told the group the sad news, "…. he died." Tom looked intently into each person's eyes, "He died trying to save the little girl. Then Harley risked his life trying to save them both."

"You can explain further, if you wish Harley," said Tom as he gestured to Harley, "I give you Vivian's hero."

"No Tom.   Raj was the real hero. Thanks for acknowledging me too," said Harley. "I am very thankful, that we made it to the tank. I will never forget the pleading in Raj's eyes to save the child. He would not give up on her. He gave his life to save her." Harley's eyes were fixed on the little girl. He looked down suddenly.

There was deadly silence.

Rebecca was so very grateful she was suddenly overwhelmed with gratitude as she realized that her neighbours had compassion for them. They had sacrificed a lot to look after them. She had not understood the true dangers of the approaching fires. Terror and fear had made her irrational. She wanted to give thanks but English failed her. She began to pray in Spanish.

"Pashe Nuestro Santo…"

Jessica wiped the tears from her face and unscrewed the teat from Benny's bottle, stuck it under her nose, thankfully it was still fresh. Closing the bottle she propped it up for him and checked his nappy. She was relieved to see a large tube of Aloe Vera that would come in handy later treating Harley and Rebecca's burns.

While Rebecca was distracted Jessica looked at her legs. She was worried when she saw the red line that streaked up from an old gash in her leg. Rebecca must've injured herself a few days ago and not realized she needed medical help.

"She has a serious infection," Jessica muttered to herself as she glanced across to Benny who was now sleeping soundly. Safe in his make shift bed.

Jessica placed clean wet nappy liners on Rebecca's burnt arms. She knew Rebecca had no feeling in her legs so she wouldn't be suffering any pain from them. She applied Aloe Vera and covered the wound. They were second-degree burns, could even be third. Care had to be taken not to break the blisters. She went to put her hands up to Rebecca's brow to check for fever. Rebecca pulled herself back in fear. Jessica had already slapped her and she wasn't about to be slapped again.

"I'm so sorry I just want to help you. I should have been a better neighbour, I was so wrapped up in my own world I never once thought about how you were managing on your own with Vivian." A tear rolled down her face. "Can you find it in your heart to forgive me? I want to help you both will you allow me?"

Once she had done what she could for Rebecca she turned to Harley, "You're next." But he said, "Not yet, I just need some time to sit with Tom." He does not look well.

Tom had earlier snapped at Jessica, when she would not let go of young Benny.

"We have to help each other, if we want to survive," he now realized that it was all due to extreme stress of the ordeal they had just been through. He apologized softly to Jessica.

She noticed that Harley had severe blisters and that his tattoos were destroyed. She wondered how this would affect his ego. She mentioned this.

Harley hung his head, shrugged his shoulders, "I'm alive but I don't deserve to be, I haven't been a nice person, Raj should be alive, not me. He was a very good man."

While Jessica attended to his burns Harley's thoughts were so guilt ridden he could hardly bare it. He was nothing more than a deceitful coward He didn't deserve the kindness these people were showing him. He felt like he could burst with the pressure of this knowledge and how he deceived these wonderful people, he'd never met people like this and wondered if he had met them in his earlier years how different his life would have been. He just needed to know that someone cared if he lived or died, that was all he had ever wanted, a feeling that he mattered! To be loved, to belong. The thought of carrying this burden all his life was unbearable. All this was his fault. One person had already lost his life! His throat tightened and it was difficult to swallow.

He felt a tremble run through his body as he realized the truth of his own words.

CHAPTER 21   WHERE ARE THE CHICKENS?

Vivian suddenly asked, "Where are my Chickens?"

Everyone started to laugh, breaking the tension for a moment.

Tom said to Vivian, "I think they may be hiding at the creek. We will have a look later."

"Ok" came Vivian's reply.

She wanted to ask Raj where her chickens were but she couldn't see him there.

She had told him where some of her chickens were; one on top of the tree and there was one around at the water and also some were running away from the fire.

Vivian worried about her chickens.

'Maybe the nice man is looking for my chickens now,' she suddenly thought and felt better.

The little girl snuggled into her grandmother. "I love you" she smiled.

All fell silent again.

Tom saw one of Lilly's crochet blankets in the groups' supplies. He started to reflect on the joys he and Lilly had shared as they raised their own little family. He missed her. He suddenly felt a massive pang in his heart, Lilly was, his one true love. So many good memories of her came flooding in.

Then the painful questions invaded his loving thoughts.

'Where was she?'

'Did she get to a safe place to wait out the horrible fire?'

'What about her Christmas shopping?'

'Will there even be a home left, to come back too?'

'Will I even be alive if she does return?'

Tom felt a little uptight and seemed to breathe with difficulty he sat down on a chair partially submerged in the filthy water and hoped the feeling would pass.

'It's all the excitement and rushing,' he thought, *'I'll be right.'*

*****

The words of love brought Jessica's fears to the surface.

'Benny needs his daddy.'

'Where is Matthew?'

'I hope he left late and didn't get caught in the fire?'

'Please let him be safe.'

She looked across at Benny and wondered what was going to happen to them if anything happened to Matthew. The little boy loved his Dad so much.

'When was this nightmare going to end?'

Harley's shout broke into her thoughts, "Hey the old guys looking crook. What's wrong with him?"

Jessica sloshed over to Tom as rapidly as she could.

Tom whispered shakily, "It's all too much."

The nurse stated softly as she placed her hand reassuringly on his back, "You're having a panic attack."

CHAPTER 22   CHRISTMAS IS COMING

Vivian was listening to all the noises outside. She turned to her Grandmother and asked, "What is going on? It sounds like a train outside."

Her grandmother saw she is scared and told her a story.

"Don't worry about the noise it is fire crackers for Christmas. Remember Christmas is coming, it is a time for celebration."

Vivian was happy for now and sat quietly and listened. Then asked again about the noise.

"Well my little one," her Grandmother lied, "They are letting them off on a special train carrying fire crackers for Christmas."

Rebecca didn't want Vivian to be afraid. She was just a small girl and she couldn't possibly understand that they were likely to die soon. She was so happy to be celebrating Christmas. Rebecca held her tight and hoped if they have to die at least her little angel goes blissfully unaware.

Meanwhile, Tom's thoughts returned, he hoped that Raj had submerged the gas bottles and the petrol containers in the creek.

Tom had shown Raj how to disconnect Jessica's bottle, before they had gone over to look at his water tank. 'I hope he buried them all,' he smiled as he remembered Raj's exuberance and dedication to the task.

Now Tom felt the strain and found himself a little breathless as he gasped for air once again. He remembered Jessica's instructions on handling the problem. He then began to take some deep breathes in, slowly releasing them out again. He instantly felt better.

A series of mighty explosions burst through the raging noise of the fire.

Tom tried to explain to Jessica and Harley the distance of the water tank to the area in the creek where the exploding gas bottles were located. The fire front was nearly over them now. The foul smell of the water was overpowering, but they felt that it was better to submerge further than be roasted alive. At least this way, they might have a slim chance of surviving.

Benny woke up screaming. He quickly sat up, frightened by the increasing sound rushing toward them. He looked to his mother for reassurance.

Vivian had a shocked look on her face after the first explosion but Rebecca quickly adapted her story about a train now coming up the mountain, to hide the truth. Then there were the loud bangs all the adults looked from one to the other. Rebecca bless her, wove the noise into the story. She said, "The train is bringing some wonderful fireworks big red and green ones and they are just trying some to make sure they are going to work. We will see all of them on New Year's Eve."

Tom wasn't at all sure they'd see New Year's Eve ever again.

Rebecca chirped, her voice rasping with dryness, telling her little one a great story as she distracted her from the agents of death that were now surrounding them.

Benny had soon become captivated by the sound of Rebecca's voice.

Jessica was finally able to talk to Harley. She knew he was struggling with the loss of Raj. She needed to distract him. She tugged Harley's shirt, she asked him quietly "Can you check that pipe up there and see if you can see what is happening outside?"

Harley went over to where she had pointed. It was the main pipe, which would once have brought rainwater into the tank. He looked through the pipe and what he saw will live with him forever. It was a wall of fire rushing toward them at an alarming rate. He had just turned around to tell Jessica what was happening when suddenly baby rats taking shelter from the fire ran through the hole and down his arm that had pressed against the opening.

Harley tried to brush the rats off his body they leapt into the water. By the time he got to Jessica he was as white as a sheet.

Harley whispered in her ear, "The heat coming off the wall is incredible and the water near the edge is heating up."

Tom overheard and said, "Huddle in the middle, the only chance we have is to get everyone right down into the water."

Jessica felt sick she had seen the rats drop into the water but Tom had a fabulous idea.

"I will get the blankets we can wet them and wrap ourselves in them before we get further down into the water to reduce the heat. We will be protected from anything that is in there by the blankets," said Harley. He took wet blankets over to Jessica and Tom.

Jessica whispered quietly into the old woman's ear. She drew a deep breath and told her grand daughter, they were about to play a special game, which involved bobbing down in the water.

Harley dropped the blankets into the horrible water. He lifted them and wrapped Vivian and Rebecca. He wrapped Vivian first. He left a large piece to go over her head at the last moment. He gently helped her into the water.

Jessica took the old woman's lead, "Now Vivian I need your help getting Grandma to play our game. Help me slip Grandma in the water."

The little girl looked confused by this sudden desire to play a new game in the stinky water but decided if Grandma was playing then so was she. Vivian followed Jessica's instructions and before long the old woman was wrapped in blankets and submerged with her little granddaughter wrapped in with her and supporting her as she floated in the dark filthy pool. Harley moved across to help prop her up. He apologized to Rebecca but he had to tie her into one of Jessica's chairs and carefully laid it on the side. He had to prop up her head so she wouldn't drown, but he was worried if he did it wrong he might strangle her.

Rebecca still detested this young man but if she wanted to survive she would have to accept his help and be thankful.

The others followed suit and Jessica cradled Benny in a wad of wet blankets. Benny started to kick and cry, his mother continued regardless.

The adults exchanged glances and felt the finality of their circumstances as the water embraced them.

The air was becoming thin and the smoke irritated and burnt their eyes.

"What was that?"

They looked at each other with fear in their hearts as the sound roared closer and then they realized it was the approaching fire.

It became louder and louder and suddenly it was overhead the temperature was rising alarmingly rapidly.

"It must be pretty close," Harley said.

Suddenly there were the additional sounds of the cracking limbs falling from trees, smashing windows from the house nearby and the Christmas crackers that they would now never use made it sound like new years eve, they had visions of a lost Christmas with no celebrations.

Jessica suggested that they go as deep as possible into the water and keep the blankets wet over their heads by bobbing their heads down under the water to rewet them, as the heat was becoming extremely uncomfortable and drying the wet towels quickly.

The strong winds had sucked most of the oxygen out of the air and breathing was becoming increasingly difficult.

Harley supported Rebecca in the water helping her and her precious granddaughter preventing her from sliding below the surface permanently.

Everyone was gasping for air and extremely fearful of what may happen. The old farmer saw the two families struggling. He placed his hand on Harley's shoulder reassuringly. The youth felt Tom's approval and placed his spare hand on top of the old man's hand in thanks. He felt a sudden lift in his spirits and wished all the more to live through this.

They all felt like this was the end for them what else could possibly happen?

CHAPTER 23   SNAKES ALIVE

Harley glanced at the peephole he could see the fire front raging towards them. They all held hands they knew they had little hope of surviving. At this moment they were closer than they had ever been. The water was getting very warm and they feared they would be cooked alive.

It was a struggle to breathe. The noise was unbearable, and the acrid smell of smoke permeated the already depleted air, making their noses and throats burn with every breath. The taste was in their mouths making them want to dry retch.

It was painful to keep their eyes open and they were all extremely concerned for the two children.

Suddenly something caught Harley's eye, he blinked in pain and there was a snake slithering through the hole. It dropped into the water and swam around them. He didn't say a word; he couldn't possibly put them through any more fear. Then a dead rat floated past him. The water was already so contaminated and smelly. How much more could they bare?

Harley rearranged his wet blanket back over his head and felt the snake in its folds. It had been curled up on the edge of his blanket. He went to flick it off and it wrapped itself around his arm, he instinctively screamed. He knew Australia had some of the most deadly snakes in the world the thought of an encounter was one of the few things that used to terrify him but right now he was beyond caring.

Heads popped out from under wet blankets to see what had happened to him. He reassured them he was all right. Through the pain of dried eyes no one noticed the snake. He managed to get the snake off his arm preparing to kill it but it got away and slipped into the water. He threw his blanket over it quickly and bundled it up then hastily stuffed it into a disused bag.

"Hurry" Jessica yelled, "Before you are cooked in the heat!"

He quickly grabbed another blanket and rejoined the group.

An incredible noise that sounded worse than explosions going off echoed through the tank eerily. Tom knew that the oil in the eucalyptus tree leaves were exploding and causing more heat, with the rapid fires becoming unbearable.

Tom was thinking, *'We've got Buckley's, we're going to die anyway! The oxygen is disappearing; my eyes are dry and stinging. My lips are cracked and bleeding and it hurts when I gasp for breath.'* Fear was taking over. *'Oh! Let me die.'* A sudden thought flashed into his mind, *'Harley needs me now. He needs a father. Can I possibly give this troubled young man a few precious years, just enough to set him straight, or is this it?'*

He knew that he must stay solid and overcome his own

fear, to help this group get through their fears.

Jessica broke into his thoughts saying, "Tom take a drink from your water bottle." He was grateful for a most welcome relief. She then asked if he was okay?

"Yes," he replied, holding his chest, "but I may need help when this fire is over, as the pain keeps coming and going."

Rebecca embraced her charge. All she really understood that they were all in serious danger.

'It is going to be so hard to get out of the water tank,' Rebecca pondered, *'...if we survive.'*

The rats tried to scamper onto Rebecca's blanket she brushed them off and felt very afraid. It was too much struggle for them to survive. She recited the Spanish version of the Lord's Prayer in her head, as she tried to hold on to hope.

Harley looked to the old woman and little girl regretting his behavior towards them. He owed it to them to get them out of here alive.

The rats keep scampering over their wet blankets.

"It is smelly," said Vivian innocently.

CHAPTER 24   TOO HOT TO HANDLE

"Where is the train going Grandma?" asked Vivian.

Jessica poked her head out from under the wet blanket. The little girl was right, the sound of the fire was receding. They were still coughing and rubbing their eyes as they sat in the unbearably hot water. Their skin was burning.

"Wow that was a mighty big fire," Tom muttered in disbelief.

"A big fire?"

"A big fire?" Vivian asked again.

"Why you don't tell me granny? There was a fire."

"Because I don't want to scare you. You wouldn't understand. You are too small for worrying."

There were sighs of relief from everyone in the water tank.

The old farmer suggested that someone should go up the ladder urgently because if the building above collapsed over the tank opening they'd be trapped for good and no one would even know where they were.

The young man looked to the only way out, the ladder. His only thought was to try to get his friends out of there; they had just about given up any hope of surviving. *'How were they going to get out? Give me the strength to do what I have to do.'*

As he reached for the ladder with his wet towel Tom suddenly yelled "Don't use a wet towel, heat travels quickly through the moisture. Use a dry one instead."

Taking a dry towel from the bag of towels propped up on the pile, Harley grabbed the first rung of the ladder and held his breathe. Even through the many layers of towel he felt the heat from the rung radiate.

'Please let the lid open easily as I have no one to help me.'

"Bloody hell that is hot, we are going to have to be very careful!"

He made his way to the top of the ladder.

He gave the lid a hard push but it was stuck, he tried again with all his might, the same result.

"Harley," Jessica said, "I can help you push maybe both of us can do it together."

Benny clung fiercely to his mother he didn't want to let go. She swallowed hard and tugged him from her, their lives were still in the balance, there was no time to waste. Jessica passed Benny reluctantly into the old man's arthritic hands.

She wrapped her own hands in dry towels and hastily joined Harley.

"Okay, lets give it a go." he said his eyes blazing with determination.

They heaved and pushed as hard as they could trembling with the effort. The lid resisted, by now they should've been dripping with sweat and putrid water but the hot smoky air was drying them off quickly.

They were not strong enough; they couldn't make the lid budge. Suddenly there was a huge noise it sounded like half the house had collapsed. Adrenaline kicked in. Jessica gave a grunt and they both heaved once again. This time the lid moved to one side, and they breathed a breath of smoky smelling air, which seemed a little better than the stagnant smell in the tank but started them both coughing again.

They poked their heads through the hole and were shocked to see the house beside them had gone.

Jessica put her thoughts into words, "Harley we need to get everyone out of here, **now**!"

"Who's first?"

Jessica had to think. The children were her first priority. They couldn't leave them on their own amongst the many fires that still blazed or on the ground littered in cinders. Jessica tried to weigh it up.

Harley interrupted her thoughts, "I think we should get Tom out first, he is really having difficulty breathing and he could cope better outside than Rebecca. He can mind the children while we get the old woman out."

Jessica's stomach seized tight, as suddenly it hit her that little Benny had to be placed in Tom's care in this scene from hell. She couldn't argue though what choice did she have. She pushed the dire feelings aside and climbed back down to tell Tom of their plan.

It nearly broke her heart as Benny sobbed and held out his chubby little hands to be picked up.

Rebecca took Benny from Tom and held both children close to her. The old man started to make his way across the tank.

Rebecca looked up to see Jessica's burning glare at her and attempted a reassuring nod as she realized the young mother did not trust her with her baby anymore either and rightly so. She passed Benny gently into the old woman's arms. They exchanged another glance. They both understood the massive leap of faith Jessica was taking by entrusting the care of her baby to the old woman again.

Jessica turned to Tom burying her animosity and focused again on their survival.

"Can you climb up the ladder with help?" Jessica asked as

she guided him towards the ladder.

He grabbed a couple of dry towels to help him get up the ladder. With a lot of difficulty and Jessica directly behind him in case he lost his grip. He made his way to the top. He finally reached Harley above and was pulled to safety. Tom rolled out of the tank onto the hot ashy ground.

He was shocked to see his house had gone.

Tom said, "I'll clear the way out and find somewhere safe outside."

Jessica didn't want to leave Benny down in the smoke filled tank with the crippled old woman any longer than she had to but she couldn't let Tom make his way through the ashen mess alone. She told Harley what she was thinking.

"Go ahead Jessica I have to get Rebecca untied. I'll watch out for your son."

He went over to the old lady who was coughing and struggling to free herself.

Tom and Jessica could hardly see through the smoke. They felt their way cautiously past the burnt out back stairs.

They were not prepared for the level of devastation that greeted them.

The fire had left little untouched everything standing was black and the ground was covered in hot white ash it warmed their feet through their shoes. Some smoke still wafted through the air. It was the trees that Jessica couldn't believe. The fire had scorched the outsides black but the insides were still full of flames brilliant against the black sky. Sparks were leaping high into the night sky.

A couple of pathetic little rats that thought that they were safe in their habitat were now little blackened carcasses. There was an eerie silence in the wake of the roaring fire. It felt like they were in the presence of a funeral, which it was for these blessed godly creatures.

Tom yelled excitedly, "Look! I don't believe it, there is some untouched grass over there."

Jessica sighed with relief.

"You go and get the children. I will make sure the fire doesn't touch this little haven."

Jessica made her way down into the tank she informed them they'd found a safe place.

She turned to Rebecca as she gladly embraced Benny, "We will take Vivian and Benny up now and Tom will look after them. Then we will come back and get you out."

It was her turn to trust the young mother with her precious granddaughter again. The old woman just stared at her almost devoid of emotion, as if she'd accepted this was the end.

Jessica turned away and automatically wrapped a couple

of wet towels around Benny placing one loosely across his mouth and nose to reduce the smoky air he'd breathe. She bent down and wrapped wet towels around Vivian too.

Harley gave Rebecca a look of desperation the water had made the rope swell and he couldn't get the knots undone.

"I'll be back soon, we'll take the children to Tom quickly," Harley reassured Rebecca as he reached down to pick up Vivian.

Vivian pulled away quickly gripping tightly to her grandmother and screaming, "I'm not going with the bad man. He's very bad." She kicked him furiously in the leg as he moved closer to her, "No, no, NO!"

"Come Vivian," pleaded Jessica holding out her hand to Vivian, "We have to go quickly. Come on take my hand."

"I don't want to leave my granny," sobbed the little girl holding her grandmother tightly.

"Now Vivian, my precious little one," said Rebecca softly, "I want you to go with Jessica and see if Santa has come yet." The women exchanged glances again.

Vivian's eyes sparkled and she eagerly grasped Jessica's hand and kept herself distant to Harley as they made their way to the stairs.

"Take Benny," said Jessica as she bit her lip trying to ignore Benny's refusal to leave his mother again.

Harley saw the anguish in her eyes, "We'll make it, I promise," and hastily made his way up the ladder with the struggling baby.

Jessica lifted Vivian into a piggyback style and made her way up the ladder behind him taking care to keep Vivian from touching the scorching metal ladder. Vivian clambered out as they reached the surface.

Harley felt an unbearable pain in his soul, he had done this and he knew he could never live it down; he was a murderer as well as an arsonist. What made it worse, was that these people finally accepted him, and he had deceived them in the worst way.

He snapped out of his reverie to the panicked screams of Rebecca still tied to her chair below. Harley passed the baby back to his mother and hastily ran back, he leapt down the ladder, he had to see these people out as soon as possible the heat was still oppressive in the tank.

Jessica made her way to the refuge of grass Tom was maintaining, his huge boots stomping hard upon any remaining sparks. Tom took the baby from her ignoring his protests.

He looked at Vivian's terrified face, "I need your help young lady," he smiled, "you need to spot the sparks for me so I can stamp them out. Can you do that?"

Vivian nodded uncertainly.

Jessica went back to assist with getting Rebecca out. She also needed the medicine bag and remaining drinking water.

While the young man struggled to untie her knots, he spoke softly to her to quieten her hysteria. Rebecca was frantic to get out the water, she was sure she was going to die here. The knots in the rope didn't seem that much of a problem to her. But for Harley they were very hard. Eventually they came loose and Harley gently lifted the old woman onto his back so he could piggy back her. Her burnt legs dangled down at his sides she was unable to wrap them around him making it even harder to maneuver her limp wet body.

He hauled her with all his might from the murky water onto the first rung of the ladder. The lad needed a good grip and discarded the cumbersome towels. The hot rung burnt his hand as he heaved his load from the water. Painfully he used all his exertion to heft her one rung at a time towards the surface.

"Give me your hand," came Jessica's welcome voice from above. "Now the other one. Its alright we've got you."

To her disbelief the old woman accepted Jessica's help.

Harley clung tightly to the old lady as her weight shifted when she gripped on to Jessica above. Harley could hear Jessica straining to haul the old woman through the opening. He pushed her upwards with all his might. Gradually the old woman escaped the confines of their refuge and was placed on the hot ashy ground above. Jessica and Harley buckled with exhaustion and tried to catch their breath.

"Where is Vivian?" the old woman cried, terror running across her face as she stared straight up at the burnt out house beside her.

"She's safe with Tom," smiled Jessica, wishing she knew for certain that this was true. "Now we're going to have to carry you. The wheel chair was destroyed by the fire."

The exhausted pair lifted the crippled woman carefully and made their way to Tom's refuge. Finally the group was reunited, Benny kicking and cooing with enough delight to light up any Christmas tree at the sight of his mother again. Vivian was standing bravely beside Tom with a smile bigger than Christmas at the sight of her Grandma.

CHAPTER 25   A PATCH OF GRASS

Rebecca was placed unceremoniously in the middle of the patch of grass. She lay there sprawled out and exhausted on the wet blankets the children had carried out earlier as Vivian hugged her excitedly.

"Granny, where are the animals and chickens?"

"There was a big fire," stated Tom matter-of–factly.

Vivian started to cry and said to her Gran, "What are we going to do without them? I will miss them a lot."

The old woman smiled, "We will have to buy some new chickens and you will be happy again."

Vivian looked across at their destroyed house, "Where are we going to live Granny?"

"Just pray my little one. You will be happy one day and understand there was a big fire in this place and nobody has anything thing left. We only have the most important things, our lives and we give thanks to God for that gift."

Harley stood there exhausted emotionally and physically. He wasn't in a good frame of mind, the thought of suicide felt very attractive. It should have been him that died. He felt he deserved it. He couldn't confess to being responsible for this nightmare. How could he tell these kind people, what he'd done? He had to tell someone! Then he thought of the church, and how people confessed their sins to a priest. He had to unburden himself! He had to!!! Or he would go crazy.

"Harley!" Jessica broke his thoughts. Her eyes were fixed on Rebecca's burnt legs, "We need to get some medical supplies and drinking water."

Tom was worried about the tank collapsing. "Concrete becomes brittle after being exposed to great heat. Better make it quick," he said.

Jessica placed her baby against Rebecca's crippled body. The old woman wrapped her arm over him understanding what was needed of her. The women exchanged a trusting look and both knew its significance.

Harley as though by an adrenaline rush raced to the water tank. Jessica followed him. They hastily retrieved all that they needed. The tank creaked eerily. Harley saw the fear in Jessica's face. He pushed her towards the ladder first and she climbed manically.

Another disturbing creak sounded just as her head popped through the opening. Her heart was racing as she stumbled out. Harley just reached the surface as a crash sounded behind them. Jessica instinctively grabbed Harley and pulled with all her might. A massive cloud of dust engulfed them as Harley landed safely on the ground beside her. The entire tank had collapsed.

Tom was yelling their names. Harley headed through the cloud of dust towards his voice. Leading his companion as they carried their vital haul, gasping and spluttering.

Tom instantly took the load from Jessica and she joined the survivors on the patch of grass.

Tom embraced Harley with enormous gratitude and said to him, "We are all grateful to you for being here for us. Lilly would be proud to accept you as her son! Welcome to my family!"

He gave Harley a manly hug. Tears streamed down their cheeks, it was such a precious moment for both of them.

Harley's spirits lifted, he had never felt this sort of connection with anyone, and he felt like he could move mountains. He was deliriously happy, life was precious and he had learnt so much in a short time. He now had a family, friends, love and respect. *'No one could be happier than me at this moment,'* he thought. *'Life is worth living after all.'*

Jessica lay down on the grass next to her beautiful baby; she was so grateful they were both alive. She looked towards the burnt shell of her house none of it mattered now. She just needed to hear that Matthew was all right and her world would be better than it had ever been.

"It was now after midnight it must be Christmas Day," whispered Jessica to no one in particular.

Vivian asked her Grandmother, "What about Christmas?"

Vivian listened carefully to her Grandmother as she said, "You have to be happy because God spared our lives. We were all blessed today. Our good neighbours saved our lives. Thank God for the people who have been so good to us. They are now my good friends and they have offered us such compassion. Thank God for your miracle and our lives."

In the distance they thought that they heard sirens. Could it be true or were they just imagining it. Their hopes suddenly rose as they saw the bright lights of the fire brigade and ambulance.

"It   is   Christmas,"   cheered   Vivian   excitedly.